THE DEVILISH D

The Devilish Deception

Barbara Cartland

NEW ENGLISH LIBRARY
Hodder and Stoughton

Copyright © 1985 by Barbara Cartland

First published in Great Britain in 1985 by
New English Library

New English Library Paperback edition 1987

British Library C.I.P.

Cartland, Barbara
   The devilish deception.
   I. Title
   823'.912[F]   PR6005.A765

   ISBN 0 450 40576 1

Printed and bound in Great Britain for
Hodder and Stoughton Paperbacks, a
division of Hodder and Stoughton Ltd.,
Mill Road, Dunton Green, Sevenoaks,
Kent (Editorial Office: 47 Bedford
Square, London, WC1B 3DP) by
Cox & Wyman Ltd., Reading.

THE DEVILISH DECEPTION

THE DUKE of Invercaron returns from a dangerous mission on the North-West Frontier in India to learn he has inherited his Uncle's title and his position as Chieftain of the Clan McCaron.

On his arrival home he learns with horror that to pay his Uncle's debts and save the Clan from absolute poverty he is expected to marry.

The neighbouring Chieftain is a young girl who has unexpectedly come into a huge fortune from an Aunt who married an American. The Duke is pressurised into believing it is his duty and he goes North to meet the bride chosen for him.

How his attitude is diverted by an intellectual young woman who wishes to commit suicide and how the Duke becomes involved in a desperate, dangerous situation is told in this thrilling 362nd book by Barbara Cartland.

ABOUT THE AUTHOR

BARBARA CARTLAND, the world's most famous romantic novelist, who is also an historian, playwright, lecturer, political speaker and television personality, has now written over 390 books and sold over 370 million all over the world.

She has also had many historical works published and has written four autobiographies as well as the biographies of her mother and that of her brother, Ronald Cartland, who was the first Member of Parliament to be killed in the last war. This book has a preface by Sir Winston Churchill and has just been republished with an introduction by Sir Arthur Bryant.

'Love at the Helm', a recent novel, was written with the help and inspiration of the late Admiral of the Fleet, the Earl Mountbatten of Burma. This is being sold for the Mountbatten Memorial Trust.

Miss Cartland in 1978 sang an Album of Love Songs with the Royal Philharmonic Orchestra.

In 1976 by writing twenty-one books, she broke the world record and has continued for the following seven years with 24, 20, 23, 24, 24, 25 and 22. In the Guinness Book of Records she is listed as the world's top-selling author.

In private life Barbara Cartland, who is a Dame of Grace of the Order of St. John of Jerusalem, Chairman of the St. John Council in Hertfordshire and Deputy President of the St. John Ambulance Brigade, has fought for better conditions and salaries for Midwives and Nurses.

She has championed the cause for old people, had the

law altered regarding gypsies and founded the first Romany Gypsy camp in the world.

Barbara Cartland is deeply interested in Vitamin therapy, and is President of the National Association for Health.

Her designs 'Decorating with Love' are being sold all over the U.S.A. and the National Home Fashions League made her, in 1981, 'Woman of Achievement'.

Barbara Cartland's Romances (Book of Cartoons), her cookery book 'The Romance of Food', and 'Getting Older, Growing Younger' have been published in Great Britain, and the U.S.A.

Other Books by Barbara Cartland

Romantic Novels, over 370, the most recently published being:

Diona and a Dalmatian
Fire in the Blood
The Scots Never Forget
The Rebel Princess
A Witch's Spell
Secrets
The Storms of Love
Moonlight on the Sphinx
White Lilac
Revenge of the Heart

Bride to a Brigand
Love Comes West
The Island of Love
Theresa and a Tiger
Love is Heaven
Miracle for a Madonna
A Very Unusual Wife
The Peril and the Prince
Alone and Afraid
Temptation of a Teacher

The Dream and the Glory
(in aid of the St. John Ambulance Brigade)

Autobiographical and Biographical:

The Isthmus Years 1919-1939
The Years of Opportunity 1939-1945
I Search for Rainbows 1945-1976
We Danced All Night 1919-1929
Ronald Cartland (with a Foreword by Sir Winston Churchill)
Polly My Wonderful Mother
I Seek the Miraculous

Historical:

Bewitching Women
The Outrageous Queen (The story of Queen Christina of Sweden)
The Scandalous Life of King Carol
The Private Life of Elizabeth, Empress of Austria
Josephine, Empress of France
Diane de Poitiers
Metternich—the Passionate Diplomat
The Private Life of Charles II

Sociology:

You in the Home
The Fascinating Forties
Marriage for Moderns
Be Vivid, Be Vital
Love, Life and Sex
Vitamins for Vitality
Husbands and Wives
Men are Wonderful

Etiquette
The Many Facets of Love
Sex and the Teenager
The Book of Charm
Living Together
The Youth Secret
The Magic of Honey
Book of Beauty & Health

Keep Young and Beautiful by Barbara Cartland and Elinor Glynn

Cookery:

Barbara Cartland's Health Food Cookery Book
Food for Love
Magic of Honey Cookbook
Recipes for Lovers
The Romance of Food

Editor of:

The Common Problem by Ronald Cartland (with a preface by the Rt. Hon. the Earl of Selborne, P.C.)

Barbara Cartland's Library of Love

Barbara Cartland's Library of Ancient Wisdom

'Written with Love' Passionate love letters selected by Barbara Cartland

Drama:

Blood Money
French Dressing

Philosophy:

Touch the Stars

Radio Operetta:

The Rose and the Violet (Music by Mark Lubbock) performed in 1942.

Radio Plays:

The Caged Bird: An episode in the Life of Elizabeth Empress of Austria. Performed in 1957.

General:

Barbara Cartland's Book of Useless Information, with a Foreword by The Earl Mountbatten of Burma.
(In aid of the United Colleges)

Love and Lovers (Picture Book)

The Light of Love (Prayer Book)

Barbara Cartland's Scrapbook (In aid of the Royal Photographic Museum)

Romantic Royal Marriages

Barbara Cartland's Book of Celebrities
Getting Older, Growing Younger

Verse:

Lines on Life and Love

Music:

An Album of Love Songs sung with the Royal Philharmonic Orchestra.

Film:

The Flame is Love

Cartoons:

Barbara Cartland Romances (Book of Cartoons) has recently been published in the U.S.A. and Great Britain and in other parts of the world.

Author's Note

SCOTTISH TITLES, unlike the English, if there is no son, can be inherited by a daughter.

The Countess of Scofield whose father was killed in the war, succeeded her uncle as Chieftain of the Sutherland Clan. Her eldest son will in due course, inherit the position from her.

The loyalty of the clansmen of Scotland to their Chieftains to whom they still look for help and guidance is very touching and the Scot will dream of his homeland wherever he may be in the world.

In Canada, where nearly all the British settlers were Scots, after several generations they still talk of Scotland as if they might return there at any moment.

A Scot is not only an adventurer, a builder, an innovator, and explorer, he is also a survivor both physically and mentally.

Chapter One

1886

THE DUKE of Invercaron found it impossible to sleep.

He turned over in bed and told himself that it was ridiculous and the sooner he fell into unconsciousness the better.

Then, almost as if a voice was telling him so, he knew that the reason for his sleeplessness was that there was something wrong.

It was however extremely irritating that he had no idea what it was or why it should affect him to the extent of being unable to sleep peacefully as he usually did after a long day.

It had, in fact, been a very long day and one which he had known from the moment he rose that morning would be if not positively disagreeable at least somewhat embarrassing.

However he had told himself firmly it was something which had to be done almost as if in obedience to a Regimental order concerning which there could be no argument.

When he embarked on his way home from India two

months ago he had felt, as he left the steaming heat of Calcutta, as if he was setting off on a voyage that was so strange, so unexpected, that he could not visualise what would happen at the end of it.

When he had opened the telegram informing him of his Uncle's death and that he had now inherited his title, Talbot McCaron, as he was then, thought at first it was a joke.

It flashed through his mind that his brother officers, who were always up to some prank or other, were pulling his leg.

Then as he read slowly and carefully the letter which had been waiting for him when he returned from a campaign on the North-West Frontier which had been extremely hazardous, he knew it was the truth that he was now the 3rd Duke of Invercaron.

After that everything seemed to happen so quickly that he had hardly time to get his breath.

He had of course been given leave of absence by his Colonel, although they had both known it was only a question of time before he must resign his Commission and leave the Regiment to take up the duties which awaited him in Scotland as Chieftain of the Clan McCaron.

"We shall miss you," the Colonel had said sincerely, "and although it is best left unsaid, I know the 'Powers that Be' are extremely grateful for the way in which you have been able to help them over matters we are unable at the moment to discuss."

"I shall miss you too," Talbot McCaron admitted reflectively.

"I know you will, my boy," the Colonel had said sympathetically. "At the same time, it is only right now that you should marry and settle down, for no wife would want her husband deliberately walking into danger as you have been doing these last few years."

2

The two men had smiled at each other knowing that what they were referring to was so secret that it would be a mistake to elaborate on it, even to each other.

With the good wishes of his fellow-officers ringing in his ears, the new Duke had set off for Calcutta where the Viceroy had summoned him to come.

What he minded more than anything else was saying goodbye to his Sepoys with whom he had fought side by side in dozens of skirmishes in which they had all known it was only thanks to good luck and good judgement on the part of their officer, that they had come through more or less unscathed.

Every time Talbot McCaron lost one of his men he felt as if the pain of it was like losing a limb, and when he was finally steaming up the Red Sea he told himself that no Scottish Clansman could have given him more loyalty and devotion than the Indians who had served under him.

He had been surprised when he reached London to find how many people wished to see him.

The last time he had been home on leave he had spent two weeks of it enjoying the Theatres, the Balls and the parties at which an extra man was always welcome.

He had however refused a great number of invitations because if he was looking for social life there was always plenty of it in the hill stations in India.

Instead he had spent more money than he could really afford in taking one or two beautiful Gaiety Girls out to supper and finding them alluring and very amusing in a different way from the amusement that was always waiting for a handsome young bachelor in India.

But now that he was the Duke of Invercaron everything was very different.

To begin with, his first appointment was with the Secretary of State for Scotland, the Marquess of Lothian, who had talked to him very seriously about his plans.

"I am afraid," he said, "you will find that your Uncle, being so ill for the last years of his life, let everything become rather lax. When I was last in the neighbourhood I visited him at the Castle and it was obvious that both your future home and the crofts on the estate needed a great deal of money spent on them."

The Duke looked at him apprehensively.

"Money, My Lord?" he repeated. "I have already been warned that is in singularly short supply."

"I am aware of that," the Marquess answered.

The Duke's lips twitched and he asked somewhat cynically:

"Have you any suggestions, My Lord, as to how I can acquire a commodity so desirable in what I know of old is a very beautiful but unprofitable part of Scotland?"

The Marquess had laughed.

"You express it well, and I can only agree that I know of no place more beautiful than the Strath in which the McCarons have lived for centuries, but only a miracle could make it yield a profit."

"That is what I was thinking on my way here from India," the Duke said. "Quite frankly, I am considering shutting up the Castle in order to live more economically and trying to establish some industry which would provide at least a living wage for some of our younger men."

The Marquess looked at him in astonishment.

"Shut up the Castle?" he exclaimed. "I never thought I would hear a McCaron suggest that!"

"It would be at least a practical move," the Duke said defensively.

The Marquess sat back in his chair and looked at the Duke as if he was some unheard of phenomenon whom he had encountered by sheer chance.

Then he said almost angrily:

"It is impossible—utterly impossible for you to do

such a thing! Your Castle has been the rallying point for the McCarons for centuries! I know that those of them who have travelled to all parts of the world and live almost in exile in other countries would, if it was no longer there, feel as if they had been deprived of something very precious."

"I know that," the Duke agreed, "but while with three lives between me and the Dukedom, I never imagined I would ever become the Chieftain, I frequently thought over the problem of what it entailed, and when my father was alive we often discussed it."

There was silence for a moment as both the Secretary of State for Scotland and the Duke were thinking of how his Uncle's eldest son had been killed fighting in Egypt, and his second son had been drowned in a storm at sea which had smashed his fishing-boat on a rocky coast and there had been no survivors.

Then the Marquess said in a different tone of voice:

"There is something I am going to suggest to you, although I expect somebody has already done so the moment you set foot in England."

"Actually when I arrived home last night," the Duke replied, "I found a great many messages and letters waiting for me, but I thought it polite to call on you first."

The Marquess smiled.

"I am gratified. At the same time, I find it rather uncomfortable to say what should more suitably be said to you by one of the older members of your Clan."

The Duke looked apprehensive.

"Now you are making me realise," he said after a moment, "why Sir Iain McCaron of that Ilk has left no less than half-a-dozen messages saying he wishes to see me immediately on my arrival!"

He spoke somewhat ruefully and the Marquess gave a short laugh.

"Sir Iain will doubtless be long-winded about it," he said, "but I can tell you quite simply—it is that you should marry!"

The Duke stiffened and stared at the Marquess as if he could not have heard him aright.

"Marry?" he ejaculated. "That, My Lord, is indeed something I did not expect you to say! If I cannot afford the Castle, I certainly cannot afford to take a wife!"

"That surely depends on the wife," the Marquess replied. "The lady who is being considered as most suitable to be your Duchess is . . . "

Before he could go any further the Duke interrupted sharply saying:

"Considered to be my wife? Who has considered this? And why should anyone interfere with what I have always thought was something very private and personal?"

He drew in his breath before he continued:

"I certainly need nobody, and I mean nobody, to choose my wife for me, or to interfere in any way in a matter which I consider concerns me, and me alone!"

The Duke had not raised his voice, but he spoke with a touch of steel which those who had been under his command would have recognised as indicating that he was extremely angry.

The Marquess however seemed quite unabashed. He merely said in a conciliatory voice:

"I can understand your feelings, my dear fellow, but you must be aware as a Scottish Chieftain that your people to whom you are not only a leader, but father, shepherd and protector, are more important than personal prejudices or, in this case, your somewhat sensitive feelings."

Now there was a definite scowl on the Duke's handsome face before he said:

6

"I would like to know, My Lord, exactly what you are suggesting, before we become any further involved."

"That is what I wish too," the Marquess said, "and I can only ask you to hear what I have to say without being too prejudiced."

His considerate tone made the Duke feel he had been somewhat hasty.

At the same time he told himself that if the Secretary of State thought he was going to manipulate his marriage he was very much mistaken.

There had of course over the years been a number of women who had tried by every means in their power to entice him up the aisle.

He had carefully avoided the young girls who came out to India in order to get married, and he spent his time either with married women whose husbands were toiling away in the heat of the Plains, or else with widows who were usually too sensible to want to marry a penniless Captain or, as he became later, a Major, however attractive he might be.

Even so, once they were involved, their caution and their principles flew out of the window, and with their arms around his neck they would beg him to marry them.

"We will manage," they would say. "I know we will manage! I have a little money of my own, and we will be so happy, darling, that nothing else will be of any significance."

He had however been wise enough to avoid the adoring eyes that filled so quickly with tears and the quivering lips which sought his even before he was ready for them.

He had known that however attractive and alluring they might be, the Regiment, the men who served with him, and his secret exploits known only to the very highest of his Superiors were more exciting, more intriguing than any woman could be—that was to say, considered on a permanent basis.

He had since then made up his mind never to marry unless by some miracle he could afford it, and that meant never.

In India the average officer found it hard enough to pay his Mess bills, let alone embark on providing for a wife and children.

He knew that in his new position in Scotland he would have to take on the responsibilities of his Clan and what he suspected would be a large number of outstanding debts, but it had never crossed his mind on the voyage home that he would also be saddled with the extravagance of a young woman who would be inhuman if she did not occasionally want a new gown.

As the Duke waited now for the Marquess to speak he thought, if this was the sort of nonsense that was waiting for him at home, then the sooner he shut the Castle, left one of his relatives in charge of the estate, and went back to India, the better.

But even as he thought of it he knew it was only a pipe-dream, something he would be unable to do because of his sense of duty.

At the same time, while he guessed what was coming, he steeled himself to say quite firmly and irrevocably that it was something he would not do.

"I expect," the Marquess of Lothian said slowly, "you remember that the Clan Macbeth borders on your land and their house is actually not more than ten miles from the Castle."

"Yes, I remember the Macbeths although I have not seen the Earl for at least fifteen years," the Duke replied. "I remember also that as a boy we always despised our neighbouring Clans, and especially the Macbeths because when we fought with them in the old days, we had always been victorious."

The Marquess laughed.

"You would have hated them if they had beaten you!

But you always had the advantage of having finer fighting men and more skill when it came to a raid into enemy territory.''

"I see you have done your homework, My Lord," the Duke said a little sarcastically.

"Because one of my relatives married a McCaron, I have had your history drummed into me for years," the Marquess replied. "That is why it concerns me personally that you should be in the plight you are now in, and I feel I should do something about it."

The Duke did not answer.

He merely reiterated to himself that if it was a question of marriage the answer was 'No'.

"The Earl of Dalbeth died six months ago," the Marquess went on.

"I had no idea of that," the Duke exclaimed. "I must have missed the announcement in the newspapers."

"He was an unhappy man after his first wife passed away," the Marquess went on. "He married again and because his daughter Jane did not get on with her Stepmother, he sent her to School in Italy and in the holidays she lived with her grandmother."

The Duke was listening, but with a somewhat cynical expression on his face and his lips were set in a tight line.

"As I expect you remember," the Marquess continued, "the Earl unfortunately had no other children. So on his death Lady Jane became the Countess of Dalbeth and hereditary Chieftain of the Clan."

"I am sure she will perform her duties very capably," the Duke remarked.

The Marquess ignored the interruption and went on:

"What nobody expected was that a month or so after her father's death and her return from Italy, it was learnt that she had been left an enormous fortune by her Godmother, a member of the Dalbeth family, who had married an extremely rich American but had never had any children.''

The Marquess paused before he said:

"I think he made his money in Oil, and when he died left it all to his wife. Anyway, Lady Jane is now a million-airess several times over, and the elders both of the Dalbeths and of your own Clan consider that nothing could be more appropriate than that you and she should be married.''

For a moment the Duke was stricken into silence.

He was too quick-brained not to realise what this would mean not only to the McCarons, but also to the Macbeths.

If the new Countess was very young and doubtless a rather stupid young woman, for her to be a multi-million-airess without the help and guidance of a man with the authority of a husband, would be disastrous.

With such a fortune there would undoubtedly be a large number of applicants for the post, but knowing the elders of his own Clan and their Macbeth counterparts, he could imagine them shaking their grey heads at the perils and pitfalls that would be waiting for their young Chieftain.

While it was obvious he himself would gain enor-mously from such a marriage, she would in turn have the security of a Scottish husband who was at least trustworthy and in whose veins ran the same sort of blood as in her own.

The Marquess, watching the Duke's face, knew what he was thinking and he said:

"Iain McCaron has been to see me, and so has Duncan Macbeth with two other relatives of the young Countess. They were almost frantic in their anxiety about what should be done.''

"I should have thought they were very pleased,'' the Duke said cynically.

"They were pleased from one point of view," the Marquess agreed. "At the same time, they were terrified because Jane is so young and has been, I understand, educated in a Convent, that she might be swept away from them by the first young man who takes her fancy."

"He might prove to be an excellent husband, and even if he was not Scottish, might be prepared to settle in our native land," the Duke remarked.

Even as he spoke he knew that he was only prevaricating and that the Marquess was quite right in saying it was unthinkable that a young girl who was so rich should not be looked after and guided when it came to marriage.

As the law stood, a woman's fortune became her husband's immediately she had his ring on her finger, and millions of good Texan money could, in the hands of the wrong man, vanish like fairy-gold as quickly as it had come.

"That is the proposition," the Marquess was saying, "which will be put to you both by your own people and by the Macbeths. I can promise you that they have gone very carefully into the excellent reports of your career in the Army, and the fact that last year you received a medal for gallantry."

The Duke did not answer. He merely got up from the chair in which he was sitting on the other side of the impressive flat-topped desk facing the Marquess and walked across the room to stare out of the window.

Outside it was a sunless day and the buildings opposite were grey with London dirt.

He had a feeling that this was what his life would be like in the future: dark and sunless without the excitement and thrills that had been so much a part of his years in India.

"I will not do it!" he told himself.

And yet when he tried to say the words aloud they would not come to his lips.

11

He was far too used to dealing with people of every caste and creed not to know that this problem was one which, whether he liked it or not, vitally concerned him as the leader of his Clan.

Of course such a marriage would be of inestimable benefit to the McCarons.

It would mean that he could put in hand all his ideas and plans which he had hoped would provide employment for the younger men who either drifted about forlornly, looking for temporary employment, or else left Scotland in the hope of finding a fortune across the sea.

Sometimes they were successful, but more often they eventually came home to die poorer than when they left.

The Macbeths had the same problem and the Duke knew it would require a great deal of ingenuity and understanding of the people themselves before, however much money was expended, they could be persuaded to work at something new.

It was however a practical proposition and, if he was truthful, exactly what he needed where his own Clan was concerned.

But it meant being married to a young woman whom he did not know and with whom he doubtless would have very little in common, and settling down to what he was quite certain would be from a matrimonial point of view a life of boredom.

The Scottish girls he had known in the past had been far from attractive and they had had little or no knowledge of the world outside the moors and rivers of their own country.

They were certainly very different from the sophisticated, amusing, flirtatious women with whom he had spent his days and nights in Simla, and occasionally a week in the foothills of the Himalayas.

They had been like exotic flowers in an arid desert, and

he had enjoyed the passionate fire they had aroused in him just as he enjoyed their wit, their laughter, and the expertise of their wiles which he recognised and appreciated.

How, after that, could he stand being faithful to one woman who would doubtless be a pleasant, hearty lass without a brain in her head and with no more idea of how to attract a man than to fly to the moon?

"I cannot do it!" the Duke said to himself.

Then as he turned from the window to walk to where the Marquess was waiting silently for him he knew that incredible though it seemed there was no alternative.

* * *

The next two days in London he was so unceasingly talked to, pleaded with, and pressurised by one Scotsman after another that the Duke began to feel that if anybody said the word 'marriage' to him once more he would strike them.

He had been sensible enough to appreciate that the elderly Scots who had broken the habit of a lifetime to come to London to meet him, were not only deeply sincere, but also desperately afraid they would not succeed in persuading him to act on their advice.

It was Sir Iain McCaron who with infuriating slowness of speech finally convinced the Duke by showing him the astronomical amount of debt that his Uncle had incurred.

"How could he have spent so much?" he asked when he was told the total sum.

"Keith never paid his debts, my boy," was the reply. "Most of his bills were stuck in a drawer unopened. I had the devil of a time, I can tell you, sorting them out, and we have only been able to stave off dozens of Court Summonses by promising the creditors that you will meet their demands."

The Duke had laughed.

"My dear Cousin Iain," he said, "my own personal assets would just about pay for the stamps!"

Even as he spoke he knew that he must listen to what seemed to everybody except himself the perfect solution to the problem.

Finally he capitulated because it was impossible to think there was any other way he could save the family name and at the same time benefit the Clan.

Almost as if he had set fire to a flaming torch, the moment he agreed everything seemed to get moving and the old greyheads hurried back to Scotland to prepare for his arrival and his wedding.

The Duke had one night off in London when he tried to step back into the past and enjoy himself as he had been able to do before he became so important.

Then he had merely been an undistinguished officer on leave in search of a bit of fun.

He found that one of his previous friends, if that was the right word for her, was still appearing at the Gaiety Theatre and after three years looking very beautiful and alluring.

After he had watched the show which was as superlative as ever, they had supper together at Romano's and she told him a little about her exploits since their last meeting.

He found himself amused, but at the same time a little shocked to learn about the men who had bedecked her with diamonds, the latest of whom had, it transpired, good-humouredly allowed her the night off so that she could spend it with him.

"I am very gratified," the Duke said. "You are, Millie, even lovelier than you were when I went away."

It was not quite true, but he knew it was what she wanted to hear, and she put her hand over his as she said:

"Thank you, dearest Talbot! It has been impossible for

me ever to forget you, and now that you are a Duke and not as hard up as when we last met, perhaps . . . ''

Quickly the Duke prevented her from saying any more by interrupting:

"I am leaving in the morning for Scotland, Millie, and I am not sure if I shall ever be able to come back.''

She gave a little cry of horror, but when he left her flat as dawn was breaking he was not certain if he ever wanted to return.

'Perhaps,' he thought, 'I am getting older.'

Whatever it was, some of the glamour, or perhaps the right word was 'ecstasy' had gone out of what had been an experience lingering in his memory on the P. & O. Liner all the way back to India after his last leave.

His arrival at the Castle was exactly what he had expected with the Pipers, the Elders and the Clansmen, who had walked for miles over the moors in order to be present, all wearing the kilt in the McCaron tartan.

The Duke was grateful that his own Scottish dress had been waiting for him in store at his Club, so that he was able to appear among his people dressed as they would expect him to be, like themselves.

There were speeches and toasts and a great many reminiscences of the old days when he had been a boy.

It was only when at last he was alone in the Chieftain's bedroom in which his Uncle had died that the Duke had realised that he had come home and everything, whatever sacrifice he had to make, was worthwhile.

He had not missed the abject poverty of a great number of the Clansmen with their kilts threadbare, their shoes or boots bursting apart, and the crofts he had seen so far were all in urgent need of repair.

The same could be said of the Castle, and Sir Iain was right when he had said it needed a fortune spent on it unless it was to fall down.

The Duke could only hope that his future wife would

15

be amenable to her money being spent on such purposes.

At least it looked impressive from the outside with its crenellated towers, its roofs, despite the holes in them, silhouetted against the moors, the long diamond-paned windows glinting in the sunlight, and the arrow-slits from which archers had once fought off their enemies.

As the Duke entered the Chieftain's bedroom where a huge four-poster bed had stood for three centuries, he was aware that the carpet was threadbare, the curtains were so faded that it was hard to remember what colour they had once been, and their linings were torn and hanging in shreds.

There were several panes of glass cracked in the windows, and as he threw his jacket with its polished buttons down on a chair and one of its legs collapsed, he thought bitterly:

'I may be making my future wife a Duchess, but she will be paying a very high price for it, a very high price indeed!'

The following day he was able to forget what lay ahead as he caught two salmon in the river where he had learned to fish as a very small boy, and wherever he went people ran from their crofts to greet him, telling him in Gaelic how glad they were he was back.

He knew the real reason for their pleasure was that he stood for continuity and security.

The death of his Uncle's two sons had been a tremendous shock to the Clan, and they must have been half-afraid when the last Duke died that there would be nobody to take his place.

It was quite understandable that they should have almost forgotten his very existence, for although he had spent many of his holidays at the Castle when he was a boy his father and mother had actually lived in Edinburgh.

16

This was because his mother was not strong enough to stand the cold winters in the more Northern part of Scotland.

But now the old women told him of his escapades when he was young which he himself had forgotten and they recalled when he had caught his first salmon, shot his first grouse and killed his first stag.

Then all too quickly, it seemed to the Duke, he was told that the Dowager Countess of Dalbeth was expecting him as her guest.

It would have been easier to ride over the moors than to drive to Dalbeth House, which stood on the edge of the cliffs looking out over the North Sea.

The Castle which had been abandoned a century earlier was further along the coast where the side of the cliff had crumbled away until it was considered dangerous.

It was only a question of time, the Earl of Dalbeth had been told a hundred years ago, before the whole cliff collapsed and the Castle would fall into the sea.

He had therefore built a house and moved into it, but the Castle had obstinately refused to fall and still stood a landmark for home-coming fishing-boats.

Dalbeth House was very impressive, well-built, and surrounded by a walled garden.

The Duke driving in a well-sprung carriage, which his Uncle had, of course, not paid for, drawn by four horses, turned in through the iron gates at exactly four o'clock.

This was what was considered the right time to arrive, and his invitation had specified that he should meet the Dowager Countess and her daughter the first evening and the next night there would be a large family gathering.

The Duke had the uncomfortable feeling that it was intended his engagement to Lady Jane should be announced on the second night.

He had hoped he would be given time to get to know

17

his future bride, and perhaps, if he was fortunate, they would find some interests in common.

He had known ever since his arrival in Scotland that he was being swept along by a tidal wave of urgency and there was nothing he could do but acquiesce with as much dignity as possible.

Sitting back in the carriage which he had insisted on having open, he thought that the countryside as they drove through it was even more beautiful than he remembered.

There was a long twisting road rising up over the moors which then fell down to a valley filled with fir trees through the centre of which ran another river in which he was sure if he had the time he would be able to catch a number of fine salmon.

Then there was more moorland and at last a delightful view of the sea stretching out to a blue horizon.

Here the cliffs rose high and he could see in front of him the sharp-pointed and dangerous rocks on which the fishing-boat had foundered and his cousin had lost his life.

Then he had arrived at the house and the Dowager Countess was greeting him.

She was not in the least what he had expected and that was the first of his surprises.

Dressed in a black gown which might have come straight from Paris, she had a sophistication which was something the Duke had never expected to find in the Highlands.

She was also, he was sure, painted and powdered in a manner which he again found unusual in Scotland, and he remembered how the Marquess had said the Earl had not been happy the last years of his life.

The Countess was talking effusively and drawing him as she did so into an elegant Drawing-Room which had a high ceiling and large windows overlooking the sea.

Everything, in contrast to his own Castle, seemed new, luxurious and certainly very expensive.

There was a profusion of flowers, silk cushions, crystal chandeliers, and the silver tea-service that was brought in as soon as he arrived was certainly in itself, he thought, worth a fortune.

He and his hostess were alone for tea and while she begged him to sample the griddle cakes, the scones, and a profusion of other dishes, she chatted away deliberately, he knew, setting him at his ease and making it very clear how much she welcomed him.

"I cannot tell you," she said, "how depressing it has been all the time your Uncle was so ill. There are neighbours round here of course, but I have always thought it important, as our lands are so close, that we should be friends. Now all my dreams are coming true."

She had given the Duke a flirtatious smile before she added:

"Of course dear Jane is very shy at meeting you, but I know you will be kind to her and understand that having been living for so long in Italy she has forgotten many of our Highland customs and there is a great deal for her to learn."

The Duke's heart sank, knowing this was exactly what he had feared, but when he was presented to the new Countess just before dinner he had been astounded.

He had come into the Drawing-Room looking very resplendent in his evening-clothes and wearing the Chieftain's sporran which had belonged to his Uncle.

The Dowager Countess glittering in diamonds was wearing a gown that would have made her seem almost overdressed at a Court Ball. It was black, but there was certainly nothing funereal about it.

With her was Colonel Macbeth whom the Duke had met in London, and another elderly Macbeth relation whose title was 'The Macbeth of Macbeth'.

There was champagne to drink, which the Duke might have expected and despite the fact that he was laughing at himself for being a fool, he was nervous and drank the first glass quickly.

It was being refilled when the door opened and the young Countess came in.

For a moment he thought she was another guest.

Then as she came gliding down the room towards her Stepmother he thought that bemused by the champagne he must be having an hallucination.

She was very attractive, in fact she was one of the prettiest girls he had ever seen.

But she was not in the least what he had expected, nor did she appear Scottish in any way.

Her hair was fair and elaborately arranged in the very latest fashion and she wore a white gown that was as elegant and expensive as her Stepmother's.

When he looked at her more closely, the Duke, because he knew a great deal about women, was certain that her eye-lashes were darkened artificially.

Her lips were certainly too red to be natural and her skin too white not to be powdered.

If this was what was happening in Scotland, he thought, things had changed very much since he was a boy.

The Dowager Countess put her arm affectionately round her Stepdaughter's shoulder.

"This is Jane!" she said simply to the Duke. "I cannot tell you how much this moment means to me, when you two young people get to know each other."

There was a little throb in her voice which the Duke thought should have been very moving.

He took the young Countess's hand in his.

"I have heard a great deal about you," he said.

He expected that she might be shy. Instead she looked up at him provocatively from under her darkened eye-lashes and her red lips curved as she said:

"And I have been longing, yes, absolutely longing to meet Your Grace!"

They went in to dinner in what was an impressive replica of a Baronial Dining-Hall.

The Dowager sitting at the head of the table kept the conversation light and amusing, and the Duke had a feeling she was putting on a very skilful performance.

The dinner was outstanding and the old gentlemen certainly did full justice to it, their faces growing redder and redder as their glasses were filled and refilled and their jokes got a little heavier.

There was, the Duke thought afterwards, a great deal of laughter in which the Countess joined, seeming not in the least shy or in any way abashed at being so much younger than anybody else.

But now lying sleepless in bed, the Duke went over what had happened and found it almost incredible.

He had known, although he had avoided them as much as possible, a few young girls in India.

They were always to be found at Government House and in Simla where they sat in little groups chatting amongst themselves and watching the young men surreptitiously.

They would blush when one spoke to them and often were too shy to say a word when they were dancing.

But there was nothing shy, nothing in the least *gauche* about Jane.

She talked, the Duke thought, quite naturally, indeed flirtatiously to him, and he was quite certain, when unaccountably they found themselves alone for one moment after dinner, that as she leaned forward towards him she raised her face inviting him to kiss her.

He had not done so because it seemed too soon, and something fastidious in him revolted at being pushed into declaring himself before he was ready to do so.

He would propose to her in time, of course he would.

21

He had made up his mind and it was what everybody expected.

But he would choose his own moment and not be pressurised into it, not even by the future bride.

Then as he turned over again, still thinking over what had occurred, still thinking of the expression in her eyes when she said goodnight to him, he knew that something was wrong.

He did not know what it was.

He could not put it into words, but just as when in India he had known instinctively, even before it happened, that he was in danger, so he knew now with a sixth sense that could not be denied that there was something very wrong: something of which he was being warned.

Without really thinking what he was doing he got out of bed.

He walked across the room and pulled back one of the curtains.

Outside the moon was rising in the sky and shining on the sea. The stars were bright and he thought for the moment it was very beautiful.

Then he knew this beauty did not at the moment really appeal to him.

He wanted to think; he wanted to understand the feelings he had within himself to which he had to listen.

He walked to the wardrobe, pulled it open, and put on a shirt and his kilt.

He was used to dressing himself in a hurry, and he was ready in what his valet would have called 'record time'.

He tied a silk handkerchief round his neck and tucked it into his shirt.

Then putting on a tweed jacket he walked towards the door.

He opened it quietly and found the passage outside was not quite in darkness for one candle had been left alight in a silver sconce.

There was just enough light to see the stairs and the hall below.

To his relief there was no night-footman on duty as there would have been in London, and again very quietly he unlocked the solid oak door, and drew back a well-oiled bolt.

It was a relief to feel on his face the cool air from the sea outside and there was no wind.

Quickly, just in case he was seen by somebody who would think it strange that he should be so restless, he walked away from the house.

He moved first through a walled garden, then out at the other end of it and found himself in a shrubbery which gave way to a woodland of fir trees.

They grew almost to the edge of the cliff, and there was a path through them which was discernible in the moonlight. This the Duke followed so deep in his thoughts that he was hardly aware of where he was going.

Then suddenly he heard the sound of falling water and remembered how at dinner before the conversation became more sophisticated the Dowager had said:

"Tomorrow I want to show you our salmon river. I regret to say it is not as good as yours, but we catch quite a lot of good fish in it."

"I shall look forward to fishing in it," the Duke smiled.

"You must also see our cascade," she continued. "I expect you remember it as a boy, and because we had a lot of rain last month it is at the moment in spate."

The Duke had not thought of the cascade at Dalbeth for years, but now he remembered it flowed from a high piece of ground in which there was both a spring and a meeting of the winter rains, resulting in the cascade which fell down the side of the cliff directly into the sea.

He remembered it was a beauty-spot which tourists

always wanted to look at when they came to this part of Scotland, and he looked forward to seeing it again.

Now he heard the sound of it like the fall of torrential rain and he came through the trees and caught a glimpse of the water, silver in the moonlight just above him.

Then he saw that standing silhouetted against it was a woman.

Chapter Two

THE DUKE's first feeling was one of irritation.

He realised it would be a mistake for him to be seen by anybody from the house walking about at night, and he had never expected there would be anybody else in the woods or, for that matter, by the cascade.

It seemed unlikely that it was a tourist and was therefore probably a servant who would go back to the house to announce that she had seen him.

He stood in the shadows of the trees thinking the best thing he could do was to return the way he had come, when the woman ahead of him moved a little nearer to the cascade and he saw she was looking down as if she was feeling her way.

It struck him that it was a dangerous thing to do, for if she overbalanced she would be swept by the water hundreds of feet down onto the rocks where the cascade, foaming onto them, became merged with the sea.

Then his perceptiveness which he used unconsciously, told him that she was deliberately endangering her life.

Without thinking he moved swiftly forward, and just as she would have thrown herself over the edge he caught hold of her arm.

The roar of the water had prevented her from hearing him approach, and she gave a little scream of fear as he pulled her back from the very edge onto safer ground.

"What do you think you are doing?" he asked roughly. "If you had fallen, you would have been dashed to death on the rocks below."

"That . . is what I . . want."

He could hardly hear the words and yet she had said them.

Now, still holding onto her arm as if she might escape from him, he looked down at her in the moonlight.

He saw a small pointed face which was dominated by two huge frightened eyes staring up at him.

Her hair, which fell over her shoulders was, he thought, fair, but seemed to catch the moonbeams so that it shone like silver.

She was so slim and insubstantial that it flashed through his mind that she might almost be a sprite or a nymph from the cascade itself.

Then he said sharply:

"How can you want to do anything so wicked and so wrong when you are so young?"

"There is . . nothing else I . . can do."

Her voice was very low and hesitating and he thought it was an effort for her to speak.

He looked down at her and realised she was staring longingly at the water pouring down from the hillside.

As if she made up her mind she said pleadingly:

"Please . . go away and . . leave me . . I only want to make sure that . . I fall into the water . . and I find it . . difficult to see . . clearly."

"It would be a very wrong thing to do," the Duke said quietly.

"W . why . . when it is what . . they want?"

"Who wants?" he asked. "And who are 'they'? Why should they want you to die?"

She did not answer and he thought her whole body stiffened as if she thought she had said too much.

Still holding onto her arm he said:

"Suppose we move a little further away from here and you tell me what is upsetting you?"

He spoke quietly, beguilingly, in a voice he had often used to extract information from men who had no wish to give it to him, but could be coaxed, or perhaps 'mesmerised' was a better word, into doing what he wanted.

The girl he was holding shook her head.

"N . no . . n . no," she said. "P . please . . go away. I will . . never get this chance again . . and you can just forget . . you have . . ever seen me."

"Unfortunately that would be impossible," the Duke said, "and if there was a hue and cry when you were lost, I should feel very guilty for not having stopped you from destroying something so precious as your life."

"It is . . not precious to me," she said hesitatingly, "and . . there will be no . . hue and cry."

"How can you be sure of that?"

"I am only . . doing what is . . wanted by . . dying quicker than I will anyway. I . . find doing it slowly is . . intolerable!"

She spoke hesitatingly as if she was speaking to herself.

As her voice grew softer and softer at the last word she bent her head almost as if she was humbly accepting the inevitable.

Gently, with his arm round her shoulders, the Duke moved her slowly back knowing as he did so, she was too weak to resist him.

Before they reached the fir trees there were a few tree trunks which had been cut down by the wood-cutters and were doubtless waiting to be removed.

Four of them were formed into a seat and as they reached them the Duke said:

"Suppose we sit down and talk about this?"

27

As if she was only semi-conscious of what he was doing, as he stopped leading her the girl looked back at the cascade and said:

"P . please . . leave me . . as I have told you . . this is my only . . chance."

"Your only chance of dying?" the Duke enquired. "How is that possible?"

He released her arm, and when he would have asked her again to sit on the trunks of the trees he realised she was scantily dressed in what he thought incredulously was a nightgown.

Realising it would be very uncomfortable for her to sit on the rough tree trunk, he pulled off his tweed jacket and laid it down to make a cushion for her.

Then as she seemed incapable of movement he pushed her gently on to it.

When she was seated he looked down and saw that she was wearing a pair of bedroom slippers and her ankles were bare.

"Now tell me about yourself," he asked quietly.

She turned to look at him and he thought it was impossible for any woman's eyes to fill her face in such a strange way.

Then as he looked at her wrists he realised she was suffering from starvation.

He had seen too many people in India on the verge of death through lack of food not to recognise the symptoms—the protruding bones, the tightness of the skin, and the sharpness of the chin-line.

"Tell me what is wrong," he said very quietly. "I can see that you have had literally nothing to eat."

It flashed through his mind that this was the sort of poverty from which the Countess's money would be able to save his Clansmen in the future.

He was listening intently as the girl looked away from him again and said:

"They . . bring me the food . . upstairs . . to impress the servants . . but they do not . . give it to m . me."

"I do not understand," the Duke said. "Who are 'they' and how can they do anything so cruel?"

The girl gave a sudden cry.

"Forget I . . said that! Please . . forget it! It was . . a mistake!"

Now there was a terror in her voice that had not been there before, and as she looked away from him towards the cascade he knew once again that she was contemplating how she could reach it without his stopping her.

"Let us start at the beginning," the Duke said. "Tell me your name."

"G . Giovanna," she replied slowly.

"Is that all?"

"That is my . . name. I have . . no other."

It seemed to the Duke extraordinary that she should have an Italian name in the middle of Scotland, but he did not question her further. He merely said:

"And now, Giovanna, you cannot do anything so unkind as to leave me curious about you for the rest of my life."

"Y . you are . . going to . . leave me?"

There was a sudden note of hope in her voice, and he knew that if he did leave her she would drown herself immediately.

"If I do so," he said choosing his words with care, "you will have to convince me that I would be right in allowing anybody so young to throw away the most precious thing any of us possess."

Giovanna drew in her breath. Then she said:

"I . . I have to . . I swear to you . . if I do not . . drown myself . . which you stopped me from doing . . I shall only . . waste away . . growing weaker and . . weaker until I am . . dead!"

"Where will you do that?" the Duke asked.

29

"In my prison . . but tonight because they were so . . excited at having an . . important visitor . . the old maid . . pretended to bring me my food . . but she forgot to lock the door and so . . I escaped!"

She gave a deep sigh. Then as if she was talking to herself she said:

"I have always . . loved the cascade. I am . . quite happy to . . die in its arms."

"It would be very, very foolish," the Duke said.

She shook her head.

"I shall . . die soon . . anyway."

"How can you be sure of that?"

"Because it is what I . . have to do . . so that . . . "

He thought she would say more. Then she seemed to bite back the words as they came to her lips.

There was silence, until after a moment she went on:

"I . . have told you what you . . wanted to know . . now please . . say goodbye and . . leave me."

"If I do that," the Duke said in a deep voice, "do you think I could ever live with myself again, thinking about you swept down by the water onto the rocks and out to sea?"

"I will be . . happy in the . . sea."

"But you would be on my conscience for the rest of my life," the Duke said, "and that is something I cannot contemplate."

"Why . . not? You are a . . stranger . . you know nothing about . . me. Perhaps tomorrow you . . will think this was all a . . dream."

"And when they tell me you are dead, what am I to say?"

Giovanna gave a laugh that was not a laugh but a strange strangled sound. Yet for a moment her lips were curved in a smile.

"Do you really . . think they would tell you . . or anybody . . else?"

30

Then as if an idea had struck her she turned to look at him.

"Who are . . you?" she asked. "You do not . . speak like . . one of the . . Clansmen which I thought . . you were when you . . first caught . . hold of me."

"My name is Talbot."

She was silent for a moment, and the Duke guessed that she was thinking of the many Talbots she perhaps knew and wondering if he was one of them.

Then in a voice that was hardly audible she said in a whisper:

"T . Talbot . . McCaron! You are not . . you cannot be the . . Duke!"

She looked up at him as she spoke and saw the answer in his face and gave a little scream.

"How could . . you come . . here? How could . . I have . . met you? Now they will certainly . . kill me . . and I cannot . . bear it."

She gave another little scream and toppled forward and collapsed on the ground at the Duke's feet.

He stared down at her for a moment in consternation, then rose and picked her up in his arms.

As he did so he knew he was right in thinking she was wearing nothing but a nightgown.

He could feel how thin and emaciated her body was, her hip bones were sticking out sharply and he was sure that every rib was visible.

She had fainted and as her head went back over his arm her long hair streamed down and seemed to be part of the cascade itself.

He wondered what he should do with her and where he should take her.

Then suddenly his sixth sense took over and everything fell into place, in the strange manner it always did when he was in danger or it was imperative that he should make a decision.

31

He could not explain to himself how it had happened a dozen times in India to save his life and that of his men.

Yet the ideas had come to him so clearly, so positively, that he had known all he had to do was to obey them.

Now, without hesitating, he carried Giovanna back through the wood and into the shrubbery, and only when he reached the edge of the gardens did he leave the path by which he had come.

Instead he walked away from the house and down through what appeared to be an orchard of fruit trees until he almost reached the end of the drive.

Here he put Giovanna down amongst the shrubs which bordered the drive from the lodge to the front door, and looking at her as she lay in the grass he thought for a moment that she was dead.

Then he was aware that so faintly that her breasts hardly seemed to move she was breathing, and her pulse perceptible though was very weak.

He had seen so many people near death at one time or another that he was aware, without asking the advice of any Physician, that unless something was done quickly about Giovanna she would certainly die.

Again the subconscious part of his brain which directed him told him what to do.

He pulled off the silk handkerchief he had tied around his neck, and knotting it skilfully around one of Giovanna's thin wrists tied her securely to the root of a rhododendron bush.

He then remembered that he had left his tweed jacket behind on the tree trunks where they had been sitting, which he might have put behind her head.

But she looked fairly comfortable lying stretched out on the grass and he thought it unlikely she would recover consciousness very quickly.

He took one last look at her to make certain it would

32

be impossible for anybody who was passing down the drive to see her and then went hurriedly back to the house.

The front door was ajar just as it had been when he left and he went up the stairs to his bedroom.

Closing the door behind him he rang the bell for his valet.

*　　*　　*

When the Duke left India he had brought with him his Batman who had served with him in the Regiment for nearly ten years.

He was a Scotsman by the name of Ross and was the only person except for a few high officials who knew of the dangerous exploits his master had undertaken in the 'Great Game'.

The 'Great Game' was a part of an Intelligence Service which was so secret that its members were known only by numbers and the actions they undertook on behalf of the British Raj were never spoken about except in secret by the most senior officials behind closed doors.

Talbot McCaron had found Ross indispensable, and he had only been afraid that now he had returned to civilian life the man would leave him because he missed the excitement that had been so much part of their lives during the last few years.

It was Ross who had said to him when he was dressing for dinner:

"They've certainly made Yer Grace comfortable! They've even run a bell from this room to mine just in case yer wants somethin' in the night!"

The Duke had laughed.

"That is unlikely."

"Well, if ye do, I'll hear ye," Ross said. "It's impossible not tae. The bell's fixed t' the bed!"

33

The Duke laughed again. He was certain that the Dowager was determined to make a fuss of him, and it was another way of ensuring there was no way he could escape from the planned marriage.

Now as he waited, wondering what he would do if Ross had not heard the bell or if it did not work, it was with a sense of relief that he heard his footsteps outside and the door open quietly.

"Yer Grace rang?"

"Yes, Ross," the Duke replied. "Come in and shut the door."

The way he spoke told his valet that in his own words 'somethin' was up' and there was a glint in his eyes that had not been there earlier in the evening.

* * *

Nearly an hour later the Duke with his teeth obviously chattering although he was wrapped in blankets, was helped down the stairs by the Steward of the household and his valet.

He was so weak with the malaria that was making him shake, as Ross said, 'like an aspen leaf', that they almost had to carry him across the hall and into his closed carriage, which was waiting outside the door.

Only as the two men lifted the almost helpless Duke onto the back seat did he murmur:

"I am sorry—tell Her Ladyship how—sorry I am!"

"She will be deeply distressed, Your Grace," the Steward replied. "We can only hope that this terrible attack will soon pass off when you are treated by your own Physician at the Castle."

"Thank you—thank you!" the Duke managed to gasp.

Ross, having covered his knees with a rug, got into the carriage to sit opposite his master.

As he did so the Steward said:

"You'll let Her Ladyship know when His Grace's better? She'll be distressed, deeply distressed, that he'll miss the party tomorrow night which is being given in his honour."

"His Grace'll be disappointed too as soon as he's well enough to know what's what," Ross answered. "These attacks of malaria often leave him weak as a kitten!"

The Steward made a sound of sympathy and stepped back as the footman shut the door of the carriage, climbed up on the box and the horses moved away.

As they did so the Duke disentangled himself from the blankets which had covered his head saying:

"You have told Sutherland where to stop?"

"I've told him, Yer Grace," Ross answered, "but it'd be best if ye'd point the place out tae him."

He looked out of the small window behind his master's head before he said:

"We're oot of sight o' the house now, Yer Grace."

"Then for God's sake let the window down! I am suffocating!" the Duke replied.

He pulled off the rest of the blankets, and arranged them on the seat beside him.

Then as the horses came to a standstill Ross opened the door and the Duke stepped out.

The carriage had stopped a little too soon and, as he walked along the shrubs lining the drive to where he had left Giovanna, the coachman drove the horses alongside him.

The Duke now moved through the shrubs, half-afraid that Giovanna might have recovered, released herself, and disappeared.

He had made the knot as tight and secure as he could, but one of her hands was free.

Then he saw the white of her nightgown and knew she was exactly where he had left her unconscious on the grass.

He undid the silk handkerchief leaving one end still tied round her wrist and lifted her up in his arms.

He hurried with her to the open door of the carriage and putting her inside wrapped her in the blankets that had covered him when he left the house.

He laid her on the back seat, and without being told Ross closed the carriage-door and climbed up on the box beside the footman.

As they set off, the Duke knew that he was doing what would be considered by his hostess to be outrageous, in that he had not proposed to the Countess.

But for the moment he was concerned only with saving the life of Giovanna, whoever she might be, and protecting her from those who she was convinced were trying to kill her.

Her story hardly seemed possible and he was sure that most people would say it was the fabrication of someone who was deranged.

Yet he was sure in his own mind that she was sane and suffering only from starvation.

They had travelled for several miles before, without moving, she opened her eyes.

The Duke, who had been watching her intently bent forward. Then kneeling on the floor so that he was nearer still he said quietly:

"You are all right, Giovanna, so do not be afraid."

She stared at him in bewilderment before she asked:

"W . where . . am I . . and why . . are you h . here?"

Then she gave a little sound that should have been a cry before she added:

"You . . stopped me . . you stopped me from . . dying."

"I decided we must save you," the Duke replied, "so I am taking you away."

Her huge eyes widened for a moment, then she looked up at the roof of the carriage and said:

"I . . I am . . moving . . what is . . h . happening?"

"You are in my carriage," the Duke explained, "and I am taking you to my Castle."

It took her a moment, he thought, to understand what he was saying.

Then in a voice almost shrill with terror she said:

"But you must . . not do . . that! When they . . find out, they will . . punish me as they . . threatened to do . . and I cannot . . allow that to happen."

"What did they say the punishment would be?" the Duke asked quietly.

"I cannot . . tell you that . . it is too dangerous . . so please . . please . . take me back."

"To die?"

"To die . . then no one will . . suffer."

"Except you."

She did not answer, but her eyes were still dark with terror as she said:

"Do they know . . did you tell them you were . . taking me away?"

"No, of course not!" the Duke said quickly. "They think, if you are talking about the Dowager Countess, that I have been taken ill with a very bad attack of malaria and have had to return to my Castle to be treated by my own Physician, who understands exactly what is required."

"She . . will not . . know that I am . . with you?"

"Why should she?" the Duke asked. "Perhaps she will think, since you have disappeared, that you have killed yourself as you intended to do in the cascade."

"If she . . believes that . . it will be . . all right," Giovanna whispered. "But how will you . . hide me?"

"I will be able to hide you," the Duke assured her. "I promise you no one will know you are with me except those I can trust."

37

He thought as he spoke that Ross would nurse her and they would take into their confidence only a few of the older servants who had served the late Duke for a long time.

They would be completely and absolutely loyal to anything their new master and Chieftain asked of them.

At the same time he was aware that there were dangers.

It would be an unforgivable insult to the Dalbeths if it was ever known he had lied about the attack of malaria and had taken away with him a young woman who for some reason he could not ascertain they had imprisoned and ill-treated.

Giovanna closed her eyes as if she was too weak to say any more, and the Duke sat back again on the seat thinking the whole thing was incredible.

It was the kind of drama he might have expected in India in the 'Great Game', but certainly something he had not dreamed of finding in Scotland.

As he looked at the girl opposite him in the faint light of the dawn, he thought he had never seen anybody look so fragile and so emaciated. She really did seem to be on the edge of death.

By the time they reached his Castle the first rays of the sun were sweeping away the darkness of the night, but there were still a few stars twinkling over the moors.

Ross got in at the back of the house to unbolt the heavy front door.

There was nobody to see the Duke carry Giovanna wrapped closely in blankets up the stairs.

He had already decided it would be a mistake for her to be put in one of the State Rooms on the First Floor where as was usual in Scotland, the Chieftain's Room and other Reception Rooms were.

Instead he took her to the very end of the passage to a room in one of the turrets which he knew from the past was seldom used unless the Castle was full.

It was a pretty room which he had always loved as a boy because it was round.

There was a large curtain-draped bed in it and as he laid Giovanna down gently against the pillows the early sunshine came in through the window and the Duke could see her clearly for the first time in daylight.

Her hair was not silver as it had seemed in the moonlight, but the pale gold of the sun itself.

Her face was even thinner than it had seemed before and he knew that the lines on it came from starvation, as did the sharpness of her chinbone and the slenderness of her neck.

He laid her down and when he bent to take off her slippers he saw that one was missing.

He removed the other and covered her with the blankets when Ross, who had gone on his instructions to the kitchen, came back with a glass in his hand.

"I've beaten up an egg in milk, Yer Grace," he said, "and added a wee drop o' brandy."

The Duke raised Giovanna up with his arm around her shoulders and when she opened her eyes began to feed her with a spoon, from the glass which Ross held close to her.

For a moment he thought she was too weak to swallow. But as he pressed the spoon against her lips saying: "Try to drink a little," she obeyed him in the same way as a child might have done.

She swallowed several spoonfuls before she made a feeble movement with one hand as if she wanted no more.

"You have to try to swallow it all," the Duke said firmly. "You are sensible enough to know that you are starving and this will give you strength."

"I . . I am . . sorry," she said faintly.

He knew she was apologising for having been unconscious.

When he managed to persuade her to take several more spoonfuls he thought there was just a little more colour in her face, but it might have been the sunshine.

Then she asked faintly:

"Am . . I in your . . Castle?"

"Yes, I brought you here," the Duke replied, "and I promise you will be safe and nobody will know that you are my guest."

"They . . must not know . . you promise . . you swear they . . will not . . know. If they do . . they will kill . . her!"

"Kill who?"

He realised as soon as he asked the question that the terror was back in Giovanna's eyes and she turned her head to one side saying:

"I . . I should not have . . said that . . forget it . . please . . forget it."

The appeal in her eyes was so agonising that the Duke knew he must not, at least for the moment, press her.

"Now I am going to leave you to go to sleep," he said. "When you wake up you must promise me to try to eat what Ross will bring you. When you feel strong enough you and I will make plans."

He thought she could hardly hear what he was saying and was finding it impossible to understand.

He therefore covered her up to the chin with the blankets, pulled the curtains to shut out the light, and without saying any more went from the room.

He knew that Ross would stay on watch until she was completely asleep.

Then as he went to his own bedroom he was wondering frantically what he should do and where he could send Giovanna where she would be safe.

He was well aware it would be a great mistake to keep her for long in the Castle.

40

However loyal his servants might be, there was sure to be somebody who, if pressed, would reveal that he had a young and female guest.

He also knew that tomorrow, when it was discovered that he had left Dalbeth House without proposing marriage to the Countess, there would be consternation.

At first they would accept the Steward's explanation that an attack of malaria had forced him to return home.

But he could not keep that pretence up for long and the fact that he was supposed to be ill must convince his own people as well as the Dalbeths.

This meant he would be tied to his bedroom, which would be intolerable when there was so much to do.

When the Duke had undressed and got into bed, he closed his eyes and hoped he would be able to sleep, but instead he found himself asking the age-old question:

"Why does everything always happen to me?"

* * *

The Duke was awoken by Ross pulling back the curtains and setting down beside the bed a tray on which there was a tea-pot and a thin slice of newly baked bread spread with butter.

"I'm later than usual, Yer Grace," Ross said, "as I thought ye'd need yer 'kip', seeing what sort of a night ye had."

"How is she, Ross?" the Duke asked.

"Sleepin' like a new-born babe, Yer Grace," Ross replied, "an' the best thing her can do, if ye ask me."

"She is sleeping—not unconscious?"

Ross gave the Duke a reproachful look.

"Ah ken the difference, Yer Grace, an' she's sleepin'. Her woke once an' I gives her some more milk. She drank the rest of what was in the tumbler as if her needed it."

41

"Good!" the Duke said. "Now I will look after her while you rest."

"There's no need, Yer Grace," Ross answered. "I slept, as ye might say, wi' one eye open, and she never stirred except th' once."

"Well, now we have to think what is to be done about her."

"I've been considering that, Yer Grace," Ross replied, "an' I thinks we should let Mrs. Sutherland into the secret. She already knows the wee lassie's here from 'er husband."

The Duke remembered that Mrs. Sutherland the House-keeper was married to his Head Coachman and he replied:

"That is a good idea."

"I'd anticipated that Yer Grace would agree," Ross said, "an' Mrs. Sutherland's already looking out some night-attire an' some clothes for when she's well enough to get oot o' her bed."

"Tell Mrs. Sutherland to let me know when Miss Giovanna is awake," the Duke replied, "and I suppose you had better bring my breakfast up to the Sitting-Room, as I am supposed to be ill."

"I've ordered it already, Yer Grace," Ross answered. "It'll be here as soon as ye've had yer bath and a shave."

Getting out of bed the Duke smiled.

Ross had been with him for so long that he anticipated his thoughts as well as his wishes.

He looked out of the window and thought it would be a good day for riding over the moors, or going down to the river to catch a salmon, but he knew it would be a mistake to recover too quickly from what purported to be a bad attack of malaria.

He therefore, having dressed as far as putting on a shirt and trousers, added the long velvet robe he wore at night and went into the Sitting-Room, which adjoined his bedroom, to eat his breakfast.

42

Because he was hungry he did full justice to the dishes the Cook had sent up, and hoped that would not be reported too quickly to the outside world.

He was however aware that they would be concerned that he was confined to his bedroom and that in itself would proclaim his ill-health.

After breakfast he said to Ross when they were alone:

"I have just remembered that I left my tweed jacket by the cascade. Take one of the men with you whom you can trust, to retrieve it, then go to the house to pack up my luggage. At the same time give my deepest apologies for having to leave in such a hasty fashion."

He paused before he added:

"Assure Her Ladyship that I shall be writing to her as soon as I am well enough to do so, and looking forward to seeing them again once my Physician will allow it."

Ross grinned.

"Leave it tae me, Yer Grace. I ken exactly what tae say."

When he was alone the Duke found there was plenty for him to do.

Waiting for him on his desk in the Sitting-Room were reports on the condition of the estate which Sir Iain McCaron had prepared and a dismal number of overdue bills.

There was also an estimate from the local builders for necessary repairs to farm buildings and cottages which was so formidable that the Duke knew that only with the help of the Countess's fortune could any of it be put into operation.

It was after noon when Mrs. Sutherland came into the Sitting-Room to say:

"The young lady's awake, Your Grace. She's eaten a little breakfast, but only enough to keep a sparrow alive, an' I thinks she'd like to see Your Grace."

"I will come at once," the Duke said, rising. "You do

realise, Mrs. Sutherland, it is important that as few people as possible should know the young lady is here."

"I quite understand, Your Grace," Mrs. Sutherland replied, "an' I wouldna want anyone outside to be aware that such a pretty lassie was staying in the Castle unchaperoned!"

It was an idea that had not occurred to the Duke before, and his eyes twinkled.

Without saying anything he passed through the door which Mrs. Sutherland held open for him and went down the passage to the turret-room.

He knocked but without waiting for Giovanna to answer went in.

She was sitting up in bed against the pillows and he noticed at once that the bed had been made with lace-edged sheets.

She was wearing a pretty nightgown which had been supplied as if by some magical powers of Mrs. Sutherland, and over her shoulders was a soft white shawl.

She was certainly looking a little better than she had the night before, but still pitiably thin, and the Duke thought that on the hand she held out to him the fingers were little more than bones.

There was a faint smile on her lips and he thought it made her look very attractive, at the same time very young.

He took her hand in his, realising as he did so how cold it was, and sat down on the bed.

"You are feeling better?" he asked.

"Much better, thank you," she answered. "I . . I thought I would never feel like . . this again."

Then he felt her fingers tighten on his as she said:

"Y . You are . . certain they will not . . find me here?"

"Why should they have the slightest idea where you

44

are?'' the Duke answered. "No one saw me take you away except my own coachman whom I can trust and Ross my valet, who, I assure you, is enjoying every moment of the drama!''

"He is such a kind man," Giovanna said, "and when I . . woke up I felt . . safe because he was . . there.''

"I told him to call me if you woke," the Duke said, "but Ross, as you will find, is a law unto himself!''

She smiled, then she said:

"Now I am . . better I have been thinking . . where I can go to . . hide.''

"And what did you decide?" the Duke asked.

He felt the fear was back in her eyes as she said helplessly:

"I . . I do not know . . that is what is so . . terrible . . I do not know . . where I can go.''

"Suppose you tell me in the first place where you have come from?" the Duke suggested.

Hastily she took her hand from his and said in a terrified voice:

"I . . I cannot do that . . I cannot tell you anything! It is . . too dangerous.''

"Too dangerous for whom?" he asked. "For you or for me?''

"F . for . . both of us . . and for . . somebody else.''

The Duke sighed.

"I wish you would trust me, Giovanna. You know I will do anything you want me to do except allow you to die.''

"P . perhaps you will . . regret that you would not let me . . do that.''

"I am quite certain that is impossible," the Duke said. "What would be really helpful is if you would trust me with your secret and let me find a solution to your problem. I assure you I am very good at that sort of thing.''

45

"I am sure . . you would be!" Giovanna replied. "But that is . . something in which you . . must not become . . involved."

"Why not?"

"Because you . . are you."

"That is an infuriating answer," the Duke said. "Do you mean because I am the man I am, or because I am the Duke of Invercaron?"

There was a little pause before Giovanna replied:

"Please . . please do not question me any further . . all I want to do is to find . . somewhere where I am . . s . safe . . and where no one can . . find me."

She paused, then she said hesitatingly:

"I . . I am afraid I shall have to ask you for a . . little money . . but only a . . little."

"Are you seriously contemplating living by yourself?" the Duke demanded. "Surely you realise it would be impossible for anyone as young and attractive as you to live alone."

As if she had not realised this before Giovanna looked at him wildly then she said:

"Then . . what am I to do? What . . am I to . . do?"

"You could trust me!"

Her eyes met his and for a moment it seemed as if she could not move and was holding her breath.

Then she said:

"No . . you must not do . . any more than you have . . done already. It would be a mistake . . and it was . . very foolish of me not to run away when you . . first stopped me."

"I would not have let you get far," the Duke said with a smile.

"I should have . . jumped into the cascade before you realised . . what was . . happening."

"That too might have been difficult, and I might have felt impelled to jump in after you and rescue you."

46

She gave a little cry of horror.

"If you had done . . that you would have . . been drowned."

"I know, but I should expect to play the hero, however unpleasant it might be."

She looked away from him and said:

"It would have been very . . foolish . . but I think actually you are . . teasing me . . I assure you this is a very . . serious situation from which you should . . extricate yourself."

"I agree it is serious," the Duke replied, "but you must realise I am now so involved that I cannot extricate myself, as you say, and am forced by circumstances, or perhaps fate, to help you whether you like it or not."

"I am very . . very grateful . . but I am trying to do what is . . best for . . you."

"Then suppose you stop worrying about me and think about yourself?" the Duke suggested.

She looked at him and once again he knew she was feeling helpless.

He smiled before he said:

"What I am going to suggest is that as you are very weak and not in a position to make decisions of any sort, you must first rest and get strong before we sit down and plan what you should do in the future. I am sure in a day or so a solution will be found one way or another, and it will be very much more pleasant for both of us than being swept out to sea by the waters of the cascade."

Giovanna gave a deep sigh.

"You are so kind . . I really do not know . . what to say to you."

"Then rest," the Duke said.

He knew as he spoke that although she had looked very much brighter and stronger when he had entered the room, now her body was sagging a little and her eyelids were closing.

47

He therefore rose from the bed and, pressing her hand in both of his, said:

"All you have to do is sleep, eat as much as you possibly can, and then we will have a council of war."

He felt her fingers tighten in his before she replied:

"That is exactly what it is . . a war . . even though you are not aware of . . it. Please . . please be very careful."

"I shall do that," the Duke promised.

He smiled at her before he went from her room to find Mrs. Sutherland waiting for him outside.

"Try to make Miss Giovanna eat as much as she can, Mrs. Sutherland," the Duke said.

"I be trying, Your Grace, and the poor lassie certainly needs feeding up as anyone can see."

"No one can do that better than you," the Duke smiled. "I remember how you used to spoil me with tit-bits when I was a small boy."

He recalled as he walked away down the passage that Mrs. Sutherland had spoilt him after he had gone to bed, with chocolates and given him snacks whenever he found his way to the Housekeeper's Room.

His mother protested that he would grow fat if he ate so much, but he took so much exercise shooting over the moors, fishing with his father and swimming in the sea that there was not an ounce of fat on him.

The same had applied when he was in India.

If he was not fighting over arduous mountainous country, he was playing Polo, Pig-Sticking, or teaching the Sepoys to play football.

As he returned to the Sitting-Room, he found himself now for the first time since he had left his Regiment thinking with the same sort of excitement that had been his in India of Giovanna and her problem.

He was intrigued and interested just as he had been when given a new assignment in the 'Great Game'.

Then every nerve in his body had been alert to what he had to do . . and the danger he might incur.

"Who is she? And why is she terrified?" he kept asking himself.

Strangely enough, the rest of the day passed more quickly than he had expected it would.

And yet at the end of it, however much he thought about the problem he found it difficult to know how he could help Giovanna and, more importantly, how he could first persuade her to confide in him.

Chapter Three

THE DUKE stood looking out of the window, feeling that his self-imprisonment could not go on and he would have to do something about it.

He had the previous evening gone out onto the roof of the Castle so that he could enjoy the fresh air, and he had stayed there for quite a long time.

He was trying to decide how soon he should announce his bout of malaria was over, and knew this meant he would have to return, if only to pay a courtesy call, to Dalbeth House.

He had seen Giovanna soon after having his breakfast and had thought there was a very obvious change in her that made it easier for him.

"When can I get up?"

He realised as she spoke that she was not speaking in the same hesitating, frightened manner she had before, and for the time being at any rate the terror had gone from her eyes.

"You will have to do what Mrs. Sutherland says, and of course Ross," the Duke replied with a smile.

"They are mollycoddling me," she said, "but while I enjoy it, I want to get up and, if it is possible, see something of your Castle."

"That might be more difficult."

There was a wary expression on her face as she asked:

"Some of your people must . . know I am . . staying here."

"They are people whom I can trust," the Duke said consolingly, "and Ross has made it very clear that no one is to talk or give any information to outsiders."

He knew that she shivered beneath the while woollen shawl she wore over her shoulders making her look very young.

At the same time he thought she looked pathetic, and once again every nerve in his body was straining to find a solution to the problem of what to do about her.

"Now I am going to read the newspapers and open my letters," he said. "Then, if Mrs. Sutherland agrees, perhaps we could have luncheon together in my Sitting-Room."

The light which came into Giovanna's eyes was very touching.

"That would be wonderful," she exclaimed, "and I really do feel better! In fact I have had so much to eat that, if I am not able to stand on my feet, it will be because I am blown out . . like a balloon!"

The Duke laughed.

"I think you are a long way from being that, but I agree you look better. Nevertheless you have to go on eating and eating until you are back to what you were originally before I met you."

Again there was a strange expression on her face and he wished he could read her thoughts and know what she was seeing as she looked back into the past.

Then he had smiled at her and gone to his Sitting-

Room where, as he expected, there was a large pile of letters on his desk.

He sat down to open them and when he had read the first three there was a scowl between his eyes which made him look rather frightening.

What he read from his neighbours and his own Clan told him quite clearly that although he had not been present, his engagement to Jane Dalbeth had been announced at the family gathering that had taken place after he had left.

It seemed incredible, really unbelievable that the Dowager Countess should not have waited for him to propose formally to her Stepdaughter but had just told everybody that the engagement was a *fait accompli*.

"This is intolerable!" the Duke muttered to himself as he opened yet another letter of congratulations and good wishes.

Because he felt he, in some way, had been out-manoeuvred and made to look a fool, he rose from his desk leaving the rest of the letters untouched and walked to the window.

It was a mild day and the light over the moors was very beautiful.

From the roof of the Castle it was possible just to see a glimpse of the North Sea.

But from the first-floor windows there were only the moors rising on either side of the Strath with a river winding like a silver thread through the centre.

The peace and beauty of it was something he had known all his life.

He stood waiting as if the scene would dispel the anger he felt, which he knew came from the feeling that he was being manipulated without being able to express his own thoughts and personality, in addition to the anxiety that he could not erase from his mind about Giovanna.

It seemed ridiculous that a girl he had never seen until

52

two days before should occupy so much of his time and his thoughts.

He should in fact have been worrying about himself and the future of the Clan.

Yet because he had always loathed cruelty in every form, and because of something stronger than himself, something which he knew had made him interfere in the first place, he found it impossible not to think about her and to recognise that for the moment, at any rate, she was of first importance.

He stood at the window for a long time looking out, until suddenly the door was opened behind him and Ross came in saying urgently:

"There's a carriage coming down th' drive, Yer Grace!"

The Duke started.

He had, in fact, anticipated that if 'Mohammed would not go to the mountain the mountain might come to Mohammed'—the 'mountain' in this case of course, being the Dowager Countess of Dalbeth.

He was a past-master at disguise, having in his exploits in India, played so many different parts that it came as second nature to him.

So without saying anything, he quickly pulled off his coat, walked into his bedroom, and put on the dark robe that Ross had left lying over the bed.

By the time he had it on Ross had arranged an armchair in the darkest corner of the Sitting-Room and pulled a screen behind it.

As the Duke sat down he covered his legs with a rug and quickly collected from a cupboard two medicine bottles and a glass which he set down on a table beside him.

Then he looked at his master quizzically before he said:

"Ye're looking awful healthy, Yer Grace."

He went from the room and came back a few seconds

53

later carrying a small wooden box not unlike an artist's paint-box.

He placed it on the Duke's knees and held in front of him a magnifying mirror in which he could see his face.

The Duke opened the box and applied a cream to his cheeks and chin which left them very much paler than they had been before.

Then with the tip of a skilful finger he added dark lines under his eyes which made him look as if he had passed a sleepless night.

"That's better!" Ross approved.

He hid the box and the mirror in a cupboard, put a newspaper in the Duke's hand and went outside to wait, his master knew, at the top of the stairs.

Knowing there was nothing Ross enjoyed more than a drama in which they were acting a part, the Duke was well aware that his valet would first treat the visitors to a long, rather boring account of how ill he had been.

He would then instruct them not to overtire the Duke by staying too long, and most of all not to upset him in any way.

He was not mistaken for a few minutes later he could hear Ross's voice speaking earnestly and confidentially before the door opened and he announced:

"The Dowager Countess of Dalbeth, Yer Grace, and Mr. Kane Horn! And the young Countess is waitin' downstairs in case ye're well enough tae see her later."

The Duke looked up from the newspaper he was pretending to read, wondering as he did so, who Mr. Kane Horn could be.

The Dowager Countess walked gracefully across the room towards him, and he saw that once again, despite her widow's weeds, she was over-dressed and over-painted.

He felt that if any of his Clan could have seen her, they would certainly have had something to say about it.

"My dear Duke," the Countess was saying in a cooing voice, "how can I tell you how distressed and upset we have all been by your sudden illness?"

She took his hand in both of hers and said:

"We have been praying for your quick recovery, and your servant tells us you are indeed better."

"I can only apologise and say how ashamed I am for succumbing in such a ridiculous way," the Duke said weakly.

"I understand," the Countess said. "Malaria attacks most people who have lived in India for any time."

"I am better now," the Duke said with an obvious attempt to be brave.

"You must take care of yourself," the Countess said, "because you are very, very precious to us. Now let me introduce a cousin of mine—Mr. Kane Horn, who arrived to stay with us only after you had left."

"It is kind of you to come to see me," the Duke said, holding out his hand.

As the man standing beside the Countess took it, he thought he seemed strangely foreign, and not at all the sort of person he would expect to meet in the North of Scotland.

"It's a real pleasure to meet you, Duke," Mr. Horn said.

There was no doubt that he had an American accent, and the Duke asked curiously as his visitor seated himself on one side of his chair and the Countess on the other:

"You are American?"

"I was born in that country," Mr. Horn replied, "but I've wandered about Europe for so long that I've become what you might call Cosmopolitan."

"He has indeed!" the Countess said. "Kane has been everywhere and seen everything. He has been very kind to me since my sad bereavement."

She forced a note of unhappiness into her voice, but

55

there was something in the expression in her eyes as she looked at the man opposite her that made the Duke suspect he held a very special place in her life.

Once again he was not guessing but listening to what his perception told him, and he knew somehow that this new development was connected with the problem that was worrying him about Giovanna.

He could not explain how he was sure of it, and yet it was there.

He looked again at Mr. Kane Horn and decided he did not like him.

The man did not in fact, look American.

His dark hair and dark eyes made him seem more Italian than anything else, except that he was so tall and broad-shouldered.

Then giving him the opening that he was waiting for the Countess said:

"You were very much missed at the family party I had arranged in your honour."

"I can only tell you again how humiliated I am at being an absentee guest," the Duke replied. "But I understand you managed very well without me."

The innuendo in his words was obvious and the Countess said quickly:

"Because everyone had come from long distances to meet you and of course dear Jane, you will understand that they expected to hear you were engaged, and there seemed to be no point in not assuring them that your wedding would take place as soon as possible."

The Duke stiffened and in a carefully controlled voice he said:

"I am somewhat surprised that you should not have allowed me to talk the matter over with my future wife!"

The Dowager reached forward to put her hand on his arm.

"Jane is willing to agree with anything you suggest," she said, "and she is hoping that before we leave you will have a little talk with her, so that from now on everything will be plain sailing between you."

"I cannot quite see," the Duke remarked quietly, "why everybody should be in such haste that I cannot personally choose for myself the moment to propose to my future wife."

Because it was impossible not to realise there was a rebuke in his voice, the Dowager shot a hasty glance at Kane Horn almost as if she asked for his support, before she said with an affected little cry:

"Dearest Duke, are you terribly angry at what we have done? The last thing we wanted was to upset you!"

"You must realise," the Duke replied, "that I am not a boy of twenty, who can be told what to do and what not to do, but a man. I naturally prefer to make my own decisions!"

"Of course you do, and it was very, very foolish of me to have allowed myself to be stampeded into acknowledging to our relatives that you and Jane were engaged. But they were so insistent that that was what they had come to hear, and of course the McCarons felt the same, that I very stupidly took the line of least resistance."

He felt her fingers tighten on his arm as she said:

"Forgive me, please say you will forgive me! I could not bear there should be any unpleasantness between us, and it means so much to me that dearest Jane will be happy with you."

The way she spoke made it difficult, the Duke thought, for him to be unpleasant.

At the same time however, almost like a flash of lightning, it came into his mind that the Marquess of Lothian had said that the reason why Lady Jane had been sent to Italy was that she and her Stepmother did not get on.

57

It was something he had forgotten when he was at Dalbeth House, but now he could remember the manner in which the Dowager Countess had put her arm round Jane's shoulders and in what an affectionate way she had always spoken to her.

He looked away from the Dowager's pleading eyes and found that Kane Horn was regarding him with an expression which could only be described as speculative.

He therefore said nothing, feeling that silence was more eloquent at this moment than words.

Then after a pause as if he had made up his mind Kane Horn said:

"One thing I want to talk about to you, Duke, while I'm here is the money Jane will make over to her Stepmother after she is married."

The Duke raised his eye-brows.

"Are you saying that the Countess has not been provided for by her late husband?"

"Not adequately," the Countess said quickly as if she could not bear to be left out of the conversation. "Ewan loved me and left me everything he could, but the house, its contents and most of his money was entailed onto Jane. Of course now that she is so rich she does not need it, and she suggested she should tell you that she wished to make over some of her huge fortune to me in gratitude for all we have meant to each other."

The Duke did not answer at once, but he knew how eagerly the two people sitting beside him were waiting for his reply.

Then slowly, as if he was thinking about it, he asked:

"What in fact, is the sum your advisors have in mind?"

The Dowager glanced from under her mascaraed eye-lashes at Kane Horn, and it was quite obvious who her advisor was, before he said:

"Jane considered that it would be only fair, as she is so

58

rich, to give her Stepmother, whom she loves very deeply, the sum of £200,000!''

Because it was so obvious that the Countess and the man whom he would not have trusted with a few *bawbees* were intriguing together, the Duke almost laughed aloud.

Instead he said seriously:

"That seems to me to be a very large sum of money!"

"Not in proportion to what Jane possesses," the Countess said quickly. "I will be honest with you and tell you that because my husband was not a very generous man, I paid for her clothes out of the very meagre sum of money I possess myself, and also for the presents we sent to her in Italy. I also helped my husband towards the very expensive manner in which the house has been renovated because he wished it to look really attractive for when Jane came home."

"I understand, of course I understand," the Duke said, "but you will have to give me time before I agree. This is, after all, a matter I should first discuss with my future wife's Trustees, her Solicitors, and of course, as I shall be in charge of her money in the future, with my own."

Again there was that exchange of glances between the two people to whom he was speaking.

Then the Countess said:

"It would make me very happy now to know that you agree, and as such papers and documents always take such a long time to prepare, the sooner the Solicitors are instructed to do what Jane and you wish for me, the better!"

"I will certainly keep that in mind."

"If you'll forgive me for saying so," Kane Horn interrupted, "since my Cousin is very out of pocket since her marriage to the late lamented Earl, she would like to have your firm assurance that this money will be hers as soon as your marriage takes place and you are in charge of

59

everything that Jane possesses.''

As he spoke he drew some papers from his pocket and went on:

"In fact, it will make it much easier, Duke, if you will just sign this very simple document, which in fact will also save you a lot of trouble.''

"How kind of you to think of it,'' the Duke said, making no attempt to keep the sarcasm out of his voice.

Kane Horn held out the paper towards him but he made no effort to take it. Instead he looked the man straight in the eyes and said:

"I think, Mr. Horn, you have forgotten that I am a Scotsman. The Scots are proverbially canny, and that is what I intend to be both now and in the future.''

"It is Jane's money!'' the Countess insisted. "She has said over and over again how much she owes me, and how much she wants to help me. In fact the dear child said only last night: 'Never again, dearest Stepmama, will you have to worry as I know you have done in the past. I will look after you and so will my husband.' ''

As she finished speaking the Countess raised a small lace-trimmed handkerchief to the corner of her eye.

It would have been very moving if the Duke had not been aware that as her eye-lashes were mascaraed, she took the greatest care not to actually touch them in case they should smudge.

"I heard Jane say that,'' Kane Horn agreed, "and I don't mind telling you, Duke, she's that fond of her Stepmother that she'd find it hard to accept any husband who was not closely in accord with her own wishes where the Countess is concerned.''

This was a threat and the Duke was well aware of it.

He leaned back in his chair and closed his eyes.

"You must forgive me,'' he said in a weak voice. "I find all this very wearying, but in a day or two I shall be able to make a decision. Now . . . ''

His voice tailed away as if he was too weak to say any more.

He was aware the Countess was looking frantically at Kane Horn.

"I understand," the latter said. "Of course I understand, and I have always been told that malaria is damned unpleasant. So what I suggest is that you just sign this paper and I'll help you by guiding your hand. Then you need not worry about it any more."

The Duke was wondering what he should reply without antagonising them into open warfare when the door of his Sitting-Room opened and Ross came in.

He was carrying a tumbler half-filled with some liquid on a silver salver.

He came to the Duke's side to say:

"It's time for yer medicine, Yer Grace, an' I can see ye're looking tired. If ye ask me, ye need a rest."

It was difficult for the Duke not to laugh, knowing that Ross had been listening at the door to everything that had been said and had come in the nick of time to save him from having to make himself unpleasant.

"Thank you, Ross, thank you!" he said, taking the glass with what appeared to be a shaking hand.

As he did so the valet said to the Countess in a low voice:

"I think, M'Lady, he's overtired, and it'd be a mistake for him to have a relapse after all he's been through."

"Yes, of course," the Countess agreed.

At the same time she gave a despairing look at Kane Horn.

As if he knew that for the moment he was defeated he put the paper he had been pressing on the Duke back into his pocket and rose reluctantly to his feet.

Then as if he thought Jane herself might prove more effective than they had been, he said:

61

"We'll leave you now, Duke, but I think you should have a word with your future wife. She'd be broken-hearted if she has to go away without seeing you."

"Of course," the Duke replied weakly, "of course I must see her, if she will forgive me for not coming downstairs to her."

"No, no, of course not," the Countess said. "We will send her up to you with strict instructions to stay for only a few minutes."

Ross escorted them to the door and as they went outside the Duke heard him say:

"It must only be for a few minutes, M'Lady. Ye can see His Grace's exhausted. He's doin' too much and I don't know what the Doctor'll say aboot it!"

The Countess did not answer, she only walked quickly along the passage and when they were out of earshot she put her arm through Kane Horn's and started whispering so that only he could hear what she said.

Ross went back into the room to find the Duke holding the tumbler up in his hand and looking at it.

"It's all right, Yer Grace," Ross said. "It's only a wee drap o' whisky!"

The Duke drank a little of it.

"I needed that!" he remarked.

"I thought you would, Yer Grace, I didna like the look o' that man from the moment I saw him."

"Nor did I," the Duke replied, "and we were right!"

There was no need to say more.

He knew that Ross was aware, as he was, that the Dowager Countess and Jane were being manipulated by a crook in the shape of Mr. Kane Horn.

This was something the Duke had not expected and he was working out how he should deal with it when Ross who had gone outside into the passage opened the door and announced:

"The Countess of Dalbeth, Yer Grace!"

Jane came in and the Duke saw at once that she had completely changed her appearance from that of the first night he had met her.

Now she was dressed in elegant black which undoubtedly had come from an expensive dressmaker, but her hair was arranged very simply under a small bonnet and his first glance at her face made him see that she was not made up.

Her lips were natural, so were her eye-lashes, and her skin was devoid of rouge and powder.

He had to admit that she did not look nearly as attractive as she had when they first met.

Only as the sun illuminated her as she came towards him did he realise that the only artificial thing about her now was that her hair was dyed.

A man less experienced in the art of make-up would not have been aware of it, but when his life rested so often on the smallest detail in the art of disguise, the Duke could never be deceived about anything so fundamental as dyed hair.

Because of her eye-lashes he guessed that her hair was the light, rather dull brown that was very much more commonplace than the fair, pale gold that her hair was now.

He had time only for a very quick impression of her before she had rushed to his side and was kneeling down beside his chair.

"You have been ill!" she said in a soft, compassionate manner that was very touching. "I have been so worried and so upset about you, and I can only pray that you are better."

"I am better," the Duke said, "and it was kind of you to worry."

"Of course I worried," Jane said. "I could hardly believe it was true when I learnt you had left Dalbeth House for your own Castle. Why did you not wake me

63

up? Why did you not let me help you? You know I would have been only too willing to do so."

"You are very kind," the Duke answered. "I was in fact, ashamed of succumbing to an old ailment that strikes down the strongest without any warning."

"That is what I have always heard, and of course you caught malaria through being so long in India. When you have time, you must show me your medals."

"I think there are a lot more important things for us to discuss before we talk about my medals." the Duke smiled.

"Yes, of course," Jane agreed, "and I know you will understand that I want to do something for dearest Stepmama. She has always been so very kind to me."

"As you were so happy at home," the Duke commented slowly, "why did you go to Italy? There must be many Schools much nearer that you could have attended."

Jane was silent for a moment and he knew she was searching her mind for an answer.

Then with a radiant smile she replied:

"Papa wanted me to be clever. And because I have learnt so much, think how enjoyable it will be for you."

She gave him a provocative little glance as she had done the first night they met before she added:

"Nevertheless, I shall be terrified of marrying anyone who has done so much as you have."

The Duke had the strange feeling that she had been rehearsed in what she was to say to him. The flattery was certainly too blatant coming from a young girl who was expected to be shy and tongue-tied.

Jane was still kneeling at his feet, and now she slipped her hand into his before she said:

"May I come over and see you tomorrow? Then we can talk over everything we will do together, and I can

64

ask your advice over some tiresome papers they have asked me to sign.''

The Duke's fingers closed sharply over hers.

"You must sign nothing," he said quickly. "Nothing at all without the advice of somebody you can trust, and who was a friend of your father's.''

"But Colonel Macbeth and Macbeth of Macbeth who are both my Trustees will agree to anything I want," Jane said. "Stepmama has talked to them, and they were so excited that I am going to marry you that they will make no difficulties about anything.''

"I still do not want you to sign anything!" the Duke said firmly.

He was thinking not of the two elderly Macbeths, who he was certain knew nothing about business, but of Kane Horn.

Then as if his curiosity could not be contained he asked:

"Tell me about Mr. Horn. Who is he, and why is he dealing with your affairs?''

He thought Jane's eyes flickered before she replied:

"He is kind and very clever and Stepmama has known him for years, so they are very fond of each other.''

She paused, then as if she was remembering there was something she should say, she added:

"I think he could help you and me to make a great deal of money, if you were interested in doing so.''

The Duke almost laughed out loud.

It was exactly what he had expected. Kane Horn would suggest 'get-rich-quick' schemes and investments where the money slipped away into his own pocket.

Aloud he said:

"We will certainly talk about it, and I am sure it will be very interesting, but of course there are other things we will want to discuss. Meanwhile do not do anything until I am well enough to cope with everything!''

"But you will be kind to Stepmama?"

"Of course!" the Duke replied. "Why should I be anything else?"

Jane got to her feet. Then she said:

"You are wonderful, as I knew you would be, but do hurry up and get well! I want to show everyone what a handsome, exciting husband I am going to have!"

She bent forward as she spoke and kissed him on the cheek.

Then before he had to find some response Ross once again came to the rescue.

"Now, M'Lady," he said, "ye promised me ye wouldna stay more than three minutes, an' it's over ten, or I'm a Dutchman!"

Jane laughed.

"No one could accuse you of being anything but a Scot! I will leave your master now to have a rest, but I am coming back tomorrow, make no mistake about that!"

"I won't, Yer Ladyship," Ross replied as he held open the door for her.

Jane turned back to blow a kiss to the Duke.

"Hurry, hurry and get better," she smiled, "and I will see you tomorrow."

She waved her hand to him again, then hurried away down the passage with Ross escorting her to the top of the stairs.

The Dowager Countess and Kane Horn were waiting for her in the hall.

She ran down the stairs towards them and Ross stepped back into the shadows where he could not be seen, but could listen.

"Was it all right?" he heard the Dowager ask.

"Of course!" Jane replied. "What else did you expect?"

They went out through the front door and climbed into the carriage that was waiting for them.

Ross went back to the Sitting-Room.

The Duke had thrown off the rug and was standing once again at the window.

Now he did not see the beauty of the moors; but only that everything was far more complicated than he had dreamt it could be.

He had already made up his mind that Kane Horn was a crook, and the Dowager was not much better.

They were certainly determined to get their hands on as much of Jane's money as they could, and it was difficult to know how he could prevent them from doing so without making himself extremely disagreeable.

If he simply ordered them away, it might be a disastrous beginning to his marriage.

It was something he did not wish to discuss with Ross, even though he was quite certain his valet had a shrewd idea of what he was thinking.

In the afternoon Sir Iain McCaron called and on his instructions was brought upstairs to his rooms.

"You are better, Talbot?" he asked.

"Much better," the Duke replied, "but you will understand that I have to take things easy for a day or so after one of these attacks."

"Of course, of course!" Sir Iain agreed.

"But I wanted to see you," the Duke went on, "as there are a few things perhaps you can clarify for me."

"What are they?" Sir Iain enquired.

"First of all, who is this man Kane Horn whom the Dowager Countess brought to see me this morning?"

"Brought him here, did she?" Sir Iain asked. "Well, if you want to know any details about him you will have to ask her!"

"I thought you would know."

"I know nothing except that she says he is a cousin of hers and apparently knows a great deal about business. I hear he has been to see Jane's Solicitors, so I suppose he knows all about her fortune, and he comes from America.''

''That is what I rather suspected, and anything he does not know about her fortune he intends to learn!'' the Duke said.

Sir Iain looked at him apprehensively.

''Are you suggesting . . . ?'' he began.

''I am suggesting nothing,'' the Duke replied. ''It is only that I would like to have it clarified exactly what this gentleman's standing is before he starts handling my future wife's money or telling her how to invest it.''

''Is that what he is doing?'' Sir Iain enquired. ''Good God, you cannot allow that!''

''I have no itention of doing so,'' the Duke replied, ''but at the same time I think it would be a mistake to have an open breach between myself and Jane before we are even married.''

''Yes, yes, of course!'' Sir Iain said apprehensively. ''And it has always been my motto never to discuss money with a woman.''

''You are right,'' the Duke agreed, ''but it is rather difficult not to in this case.''

''If you are suspicious of him I will try to find out something about the fellow.''

''I have not said I was suspicious of him,'' the Duke said quickly, ''but only interested, and being a little cautious.''

''And quite rightly so. You do not want to play 'ducks and drakes' with Jane's fortune whatever else you do.''

''Indeed not!'' the Duke agreed. ''Now tell me about the Dowager. Who was she before she married Dalbeth?''

Sir Iain laughed.

''That is a question a great number of people have asked and nobody seems to have the answer.''

''Why?''

''Because nobody knows anything about her. She met

68

Dalbeth in Edinburgh, I understand, and he brought her back to Dalbeth House to stay—or else she invited herself, which is more likely—and before he realised what was happening, she had married him!''

"Why so quickly?"

Sir Iain made an eloquent gesture with his hands.

"Dalbeth was extremely unhappy after his wife died— morbidly so, I thought—and he did what most men do in the circumstances, and to excess!''

"You mean he drank?"

"Took to the bottle, my boy, in a big way. Never been a drinking man before, but I suppose it was the only way he could forget.''

"Now I understand,'' the Duke said quietly.

He was thinking how an attractive woman had seen her opportunity of becoming the Countess of Dalbeth and had taken it.

"Was the Earl happy after this second marriage?'' he enquired.

"Not so I noticed it,'' Sir Iain replied. "In fact, I often thought he regretted what he had done in such haste. Anyway, Jane was miserable with her Stepmother, and he sent her off to Naples where her maternal grandmother, Lady Sinclair, was living.''

"You knew her?"

"Yes, of course, charming woman—charming! But very frail, continually in ill health after her husband died. So the Doctors insisted she went to a warmer climate.''

"You are quite certain that Jane did not get on with her Stepmother?"

"From all I heard—of course gossip flies like wild-fire —the girl was resentful of her father marrying again, and the Dowager had no use for another woman in the house.''

It seemed incomprehensible, the Duke thought, that

Jane now wished to give her Stepmother an enormous fortune.

He decided that tomorrow he would talk to her about it. In the meantime, he went on asking Sir Iain questions that were difficult for him to answer because after the Earl had married again he had seen very little of him and nor had anybody else in the neighbourhood.

"But surely the Dowager wished to entertain?" the Duke asked.

"Of course she did! She is the sort of woman who always enjoys a party," Sir Iain replied, "and she had them. But when I went there I usually gathered the host was not in a fit state to come downstairs, and I was not asked often, as she filled the house with her own friends from the South."

"Then she is English?" the Duke asked.

"I do not know what she is," Sir Iain replied. "It is true she met Dalbeth in Edinburgh but, if you want the truth, I do not believe she has a drop of Scottish blood in her veins."

This was all very unhelpful, and after Sir Iain left the Duke went to see Giovanna, who he understood had been sleeping for most of the afternoon.

She greeted him with a smile.

"I am so happy you have come to see me," she said. "I was feeling rather lonely when I woke up and longing for someone to talk to."

The Duke sat down beside the bed.

"You can talk to me," he said, "for there are a lot of things I want to hear."

Giovanna shook her head.

"No, I am the one to listen."

Because he knew it would please her, he told her about the history of the Castle, the ghosts who were supposed to haunt it, and the battles that had been fought against neighbouring Clans, including the Dalbeths.

Giovanna listened intently, and the Duke found it rather flattering for a woman to be so attentive to what he was saying when he was not talking about her personally.

Then he said:

"Now you tell me the history of the cascade."

"It has been there since time immemorial," she answered. "It is supposed to have appeared by magic because when the people were desperate for water one of their Elders struck the ground and released a spring which flowed and flowed until it became a cascade."

She had spoken without thinking. Then as if she felt she had given herself away by knowing something so local she said quickly:

"That is what I heard!"

"From whom?"

"People in the past."

She did not look at him as she spoke, then said as if she wanted to cover up a slip of the tongue:

"No one has . . asked about me . . have they?"

"If they have, I have not heard of it," the Duke replied, "and the Dowager Countess was here today."

He spoke deliberately, though he knew it would strike the happiness from Giovanna's eyes and bring back the fear.

"H . here?"

The word was hardly above a whisper.

"Yes, she came to see me this morning after I had seen you," the Duke said, "and she brought with her a man called Kane Horn."

He watched Giovanna's face carefully as he spoke, but it was obvious the name meant nothing to her, even though she was deeply perturbed by what he was saying.

"And Jane, my future wife, came too," he went on. "But she did not stay long. She is very anxious, because she loves her Stepmother so much, to give her a very large sum of money.''

Giovanna made a little sound and shut her eyes.

''I am . . tired,'' she said, ''and I do not think I can . . talk to you any more.''

''But I want to talk to you,'' the Duke insisted, ''and I want you to tell me why you think that Jane was so unhappy, as I am told, after her father married again that she was sent to Naples to stay with her Grandmother, rather than remain at home in Scotland.''

''I . . I do not know what . . you are . . talking about.''

Giovanna's voice sounded very weak and the Duke was sure that what she said was not true.

''You must have some idea,'' he maintained, ''since you know the Dalbeths and have been in their house, why Jane's feelings towards her Stepmother should suddenly change to a deep love and affection.''

There was silence and he thought Giovanna was not going to answer.

Then she opened her eyes and said:

''Give her the money . . give it to her . . then she might go . . away. If she stays she will . . hurt you and make you . . unhappy. Let her . . go however much . . it costs!''

The Duke sat down on the side of the bed where he had sat before and took Giovanna's hand in his.

''Please help me,'' he said coaxingly. ''I am so bewildered. I am also afraid of doing the wrong thing. It is very difficult for me to sort out what is the truth if I do not know the facts, and there is no one to tell me what I need to know.''

He thought that, despite herself, Giovanna's thin fingers tightened on his. Then she said:

''I . . I am sure there are . . people who will . . help you . . if you ask them.''

"Who are they?"

He knew she was thinking and he hoped perhaps she would mention someone. Then she shook her head.

"I cannot . . tell you," she said in a whisper. "Please I . . cannot . . help . . you."

"I think you could if you really wanted to," the Duke protested. "You are making things very difficult for me, Giovanna, not only to cope with the Dalbeths and their demands but also to help you."

She opened her eyes very wide to stare at him.

"Are you . . saying you are . . tired of helping me . . and want me to . . go away?"

Now there was a different sort of fear in her voice and he said quickly:

"No, of course not! You know I will help you. You know I will do everything in my power to see that you are never again treated as you have been. But you make it very hard because you will not help me."

"I . . I want to . . you know I want to," Giovanna said, "it is just that . . it is something I cannot do . . without hurting . . someone I . . I . . love."

The Duke stared at her. Then he asked:

"Is it a man?"

"No . . but you must not . . ask questions."

"Why not?"

"Because it might destroy . . someone very precious . . I cannot say any more . . it is . . too difficult . . too frightening."

Now Giovanna's voice was like that of a child about to burst into tears.

"I will not press you any more now," the Duke said gently. "But when we know each other better, I hope you will feel you can trust me to help you, which I know I can, if only I am aware of the facts."

Because he was kind Giovanna's eyes filled with tears and she said piteously:

73

"Forgive me . . please . . forgive me."

"There is nothing to forgive," the Duke said. "I just feel frustrated and powerless, which for me is a very uncomfortable feeling and something I most dislike."

"B·. but you will not stop . . helping me?"

Now there was something frantic in the question and he replied:

"I think you know the answer to that. I promise you I will do everything I can for you."

As he spoke he raised Giovanna's hand and touched the soft white skin with his lips.

As he did so he realised she was holding her breath.

Chapter Four

THE DUKE woke early and decided that he could not go on playing the invalid any longer.

He longed to be out in the fresh air and to take some strenuous exercise.

He had also decided during the night that he must investigate further what position Kane Horn held in the Dalbeth household and if possible extricate the Dowager Countess and Jane from his hold over them.

He was absolutely convinced that the man was up to no good—an adventurer to say the least of it. He was certainly trying to exploit the young heiress for his own ends.

The Duke suspected, although of course, it was something he could not prove, that a large amount of anything Jane gave her Stepmother would go straight into Kane Horn's pocket.

"It is no use my sitting here isolated in the Castle," he said to himself almost angrily. "I will go to Dalbeth House."

He rang the bell for Ross, and when his valet came told him to send a groom over with a note to the Dowager Countess.

He scribbed one hastily at his desk before he dressed, saying that as he felt so much better, his one thought was to be with her and Jane and he hoped she would be kind enough to give him luncheon.

As soon as the note had been despatched, he dressed, ate a large breakfast downstairs in the Dining-Room and ordered a horse to come to the front door.

He had learnt from Mrs. Sutherland that Giovanna had had a good night's sleep, and having said that he would see her later in the morning he rode round the grounds which adjoined the Castle.

First however, he galloped his horse strenuously to their mutual satisfaction.

It was inevitable that he should see with an even keener eye than he had before the amount of repairs, renovations and rebuilding that had to be done in the immediate future.

He was also quite certain that further up the river, where there were a number of scattered small crofts, he would find the same need for expenditure as he found near the Castle.

It was gratifying as he rode over the moorlands to see several coveys of grouse, and he thought that as soon as it was the twelfth of August he would be able to organise a shoot.

He had known from what Sir Iain and other members of the Clan had said to him that it was something they were looking forward to, and which they had missed during his Uncle's illness last year.

He returned to the Castle delighted to find himself feeling very different from what he had felt the last few days.

It seemed ridiculous that, because he was so used to thinking himself into any part he played, he had in fact, felt almost as unwell as he pretended to be.

His work in India in the 'Great Game' had made him, he knew, peculiarly sensitive to his own thoughts.

When he played the part of a high-caste Brahmin or low-caste Sweeper, he had learnt from the lessons his Master had taught him to think himself so thoroughly into the person he pretended to be that often it took time to return to being himself.

Now as he ran up the stairs, two at a time as he was anxious to see Giovanna, he knew that he was full of vitality and ready to do anything, however strenuous it might be.

He tapped on her bedroom door, and when there was no answer he opened the door next to it which led into a small *Boudoir* which was connected to the Tower Room.

It was also a pretty room, furnished by his Aunt who loved everything that was beautiful. Although she had very little money to spend on furnishings, she always contrived to make the most of it.

The room was a background for Giovanna who was sitting in an armchair, sunshine coming through the window and her feet up on a stool.

As the Duke walked towards her, he realised that she was partially dressed and for the first time since they had met, her hair was not hanging over her shoulders but was arranged in a *chignon* at the back of her head.

It made her neck look very long and swan-like and it seemed also to take some of the peakiness from her heart-shaped face.

She gave him a radiant smile as she said:

"I am up. Do you see? I have been allowed to get dressed. Now I do not feel I am such a nuisance to you."

The Duke laughed.

"You are not at all a nuisance," he said, "merely a worry, and I am very glad you are better."

He sat down beside her and she said:

"I see you have been riding. I wish I could have come with you."

"I wish you could," the Duke replied. "But I think that would definitely be dangerous."

He saw a shadow pass over her face as she said:

"Yes, of course. Please, now I am well enough will you tell me what plans you have made for me?"

He knew this must have been something she had been thinking of incessantly since she had woken up, and he said quietly:

"It is something we must talk about at length, but as I am going over to Dalbeth House for luncheon shall we leave it until I return?"

"You are going to Dalbeth House!" she exclaimed. "Why, why do you want to go . . there?"

"I think it only polite, for one thing, to pay my respects to the hostess I left so precipitately," he replied, "and actually I learnt yesterday that my engagement to Jane was announced at the family gathering which took place after I had left the house to bring you back here."

He saw Giovanna draw in her breath before she said:

"I am sorry, but I did . . beg you to . . leave me . . alone."

"We are not going to speak of that again," the Duke said. "It is over, it is done with, and instead I want you to tell me that you are glad to be alive and glad to be here with me."

The way he spoke made her first look at him in surprise and then a faint flush spread over the whiteness of her skin.

"I am very . . glad," she said very softly, "but I know what a . . trouble I have been to . . you and it would be best if you . . sent me away as . . soon as possible."

"That is what we are going to talk about when I return," the Duke said. "Now I want you to rest, to eat everything Mrs. Sutherland brings you, and to enjoy the hospitality and security of my Castle."

Giovanna gave a little laugh and it was very attractive.

"You are making it sound almost mediaeval," she said. "I feel I am an importunate traveller knocking on the door and asking for sanctuary."

"That is exactly what I am going to give you," the Duke replied, "so take care of yourself while I am gone. I shall be back in time to have tea with you."

He smiled as he rose to his feet saying:

"You know a Scottish tea means baps, scones and girdle cakes and I will expect you to eat every one of them!"

Giovanna gave a little cry in pretended horror.

The Duke smiled at her and went from the room, closing the door behind him.

He found Mrs. Sutherland, as he expected, in the bedroom and he said:

"I am going out to luncheon, Mrs. Sutherland, and I wish you to stay with Miss Giovanna while I am gone and she is not to be left alone. Not even for a few moments. Is that clear?"

"Very clear, Your Grace," Mrs. Sutherland replied.

"I am also going to instruct them downstairs that in my absence, no visitors are to be admitted to the Castle under any pretext whatever," the Duke said, "and there is no exception to that rule."

He spoke sharply and knew, as Mrs. Sutherland did not express surprise, that she was aware that there was something strange in the fact of Giovanna's visit being supposed to be a secret, and that he was making what appeared an unnatural fuss about her.

At the same time, whatever their personal feelings in the matter, the Duke knew his orders would be obeyed.

He did not ride over to the Dalbeth House, although it would have been quicker.

Instead he drove an ancient pony-cart with large wheels, which he had seen in the stables.

He remembered it was a vehicle that his Uncle had used to drive around the Estate and, although it was out of date, it was well strung and did not impede in any way, the speed of the two horses which pulled it.

It was not only because he was still supposed to be at least a semi-invalid that he had ordered the pony-cart but also because he wished to take Ross with him.

"When we get there, Ross," he had said when he was changing from his riding-breeches into a kilt, "I want you to say that you have lost one of my cuff-links or if you prefer an evening-stud. Go up to the room I slept in and pretend to search for it. Then while I am at luncheon, chat to the servants and find out if they have anything to say about the disappearance of Miss Giovanna."

The familiar glint in Ross's eyes told the Duke how much he enjoyed being, as he would have put it himself, 'back on a job'.

"I were sure that was why ye wanted me to come with Yer Grace," he had said, "but from what I've seen of 'em they're a strange lot and I doubt whether I'll learn much."

"Well try," the Duke said. "What is certain is that they will say nothing to me."

He was, as he expected, greeted with delight by the Dowager Countess, whose elegant black gown, trimmed with provocative touches of white, like her painted face, seemed very out of place.

So too, the Duke thought, did Kane Horn who was in the Drawing-Room with her when he arrived.

He was wearing the sort of clothes which were a travesty of what an English gentleman would wear in the country and looking at him the Duke was sure he would be far more at home in the type of costume affected by men in Southern Italy.

He might speak with an American accent, but he was sure his antecedents were Italian and his swarthy skin and dark hair confirmed this.

Kane Horn was, however, as effusive as the Dowager Countess.

As the Duke sat talking to them, sipping the excellent champagne which the Countess insisted he should drink, he was sure by the way she spoke to the American and looked at him, that she was in love.

That could be the real reason why Kane Horn was so insistent that the new Countess should hand over a large sum of money to her Stepmother.

It was getting near to luncheon-time before Jane came into the room.

Once again she looked very different from the first night the Duke had seen her.

She, too, was in black, but because he seldom missed any detail, the Duke was almost certain that a great deal of ornamentation had been removed both from the bodice of her dress and from the skirt.

It was, as he knew, the fashion for dresses, which were known as afternoon *toilettes* to be elaborately laced, braided, ruched or tucked.

After a quick glance he was sure that when Jane's gown had been bought it had been very much more spectacular than it was at the moment.

Her hair was also severely arranged in a small knot on top of her head and, as yesterday, she wore no make-up of any sort.

It was such a transformation from the first night, when he had been astounded by her mascaraed eye-lashes and crimson lips that he was certain the difference was entirely for his benefit.

This was confirmed when he stole a quick glance at Kane Horn and realised he was looking critically at Jane as she advanced down the room towards them.

She also looked at him for a fleeting moment almost as if she was asking for his approval.

The Duke was aware that all this would have escaped

the notice of any ordinary visitor, or one who had not been so vitally concerned as he had been in the art of disguise.

Kane Horn had however obviously not instructed Jane to alter her manner towards her prospective husband.

She held both hands out eagerly towards him saying:

"It is lovely, lovely to see you again! I am so happy you are well. Now I can do all the things I want to do with you, and especially explore your marvellous Castle."

"I am looking forward to that," the Duke replied, "but first of all I think I ought to polish it up a bit. I am afraid it is nothing like as comfortable as you are here."

Jane looked round at the luxurious Drawing-Room with an almost scornful expression in her eyes.

"This is far too modern and not really Scottish," she said. "If I had my way we would live in the old Castle which is the proper background for a Chieftain."

"You are right," the Duke smiled, "but there is always the danger that it might tumble into the sea!"

"At least your Castle will not do that," Jane replied, "and we must make it look exactly like it did when it was first built."

"That is what I hoped you would say."

As the Duke spoke he saw as he glanced at Kane Horn that the man was listening intently to what was being said, and he was quite certain he had rehearsed with Jane exactly what she should say.

As they went into luncheon, the Duke became more and more convinced that the conversation was a theatrical performance.

It was all about plans of what should be done on his own land and the parties that could be given in his Castle.

He was sure every word had been thought out, directed and rehearsed by a mastermind in the shape of Horn.

There was no doubt that the players of the piece were extremely skilful.

Had he been anyone less perceptive and had he not been alerted by Giovanna into knowing the Dalbeths were very different from what they appeared, he would in fact have believed that the Dowager Countess was a charming, sophisticated woman, only concerned with the happiness of her Stepdaughter.

Jane would have seemed to be a delightful young woman, on the verge of falling in love with the man who had been chosen for her to be her husband.

The food was excellent, the wine, as it had been the first time he had dined there, outstanding.

There was, however, the Duke noticed, once again far too much of it, and he had the greatest difficulty in preventing the servants from continually filling up his glass.

When luncheon was finished he said:

"I hope you will understand but I must not stay long, much as I should like to. I have given my solemn promise to those who have been looking after me that I would not over-tax my strength on the first day I felt well enough to leave the Castle."

"I do understand," the Dowager Countess replied. "At the same time you know how much we have been looking forward to seeing you. Jane has begged me to ask you to come back to stay with us tomorrow or, if you prefer, the next day."

"How kind of you!" the Duke exclaimed. "May I let you know which would suit me best? I have in fact, neglected so many things at the Castle since I returned that I shall feel as if I am playing truant if I am absent once again."

"We have been deprived of one night at least of your company," the Dowager Countess replied quickly, "and you know, my dear Talbot, how much we want to have you with us."

She put her hand on his arm as she had done before and looked up at him almost pleadingly, while Jane on

83

his other side slipped her hand into his as she said:

"Please, please, come back. Or if not, can we come over to you? I wanted to explore your Castle yesterday, but Stepmama said you would want to show it to me yourself."

"Of course I want to do that," the Duke agreed, "and I think it would be delightful if you and your Stepmother came to stay with me perhaps at the end of the week."

He deliberately omitted including Kane Horn in the invitation, and as he was looking at Jane he was aware the Dowager Countess looked quickly towards the American before she answered:

"We would love to come to you as you know, but I hope you do not mind if we bring Mr. Horn with us. As he is our guest we can hardly leave him here on his own."

"Of course not," the Duke said. "I only hope he will not be bored with what after all will be an entirely Scottish household."

"I shall not be in the least bored," Kane Horn said firmly, "and now, Duke, before you leave I hope you have thought over what we discussed with you yesterday. It would be a great help if you can see your way to sign the papers that are here waiting for you on the writing-table."

He indicated as he spoke a very elegant French *secretaire* which stood in a corner of the Drawing-Room.

"Papers?" the Duke said vaguely. "Oh, yes, I remember your speaking of them. I was really feeling so rotten that I found it difficult to take in what you were saying."

"Then I can quite easily explain," Kane Horn said. "All that is really required is your signature."

"Then let us leave it until you come to me on, let us say, Saturday," the Duke replied. "I will try to have everything ready by then and will of course arrange a party for you in the evening."

He did not wait for his invitation to be accepted but shook the Dowager Countess by the hand saying:

"Thank you so much for having me here at such short notice. I enjoyed my luncheon enormously."

Then as Jane was still holding on to him he drew her away towards the door.

"Come to see me off, Jane," he said. "I am driving an old-fashioned pony-cart which I think will amuse you."

He realised as he walked with her towards the Hall that Kane Horn was looking after him with a scowl on his face and an expression in his dark eyes that he did not like to interpret.

It was only when he was leaving the room that he looked back to say:

"Goodbye, Horn. I will see you again on Saturday."

Then he and Jane walked alone towards the open front door.

"We never seem to have a chance to talk," the Duke said as she looked up at him with what he thought was a questioning expression in her eyes.

"I wanted to show you my own special Sitting-Room," Jane said in a low voice. "Could we go there now?"

"I wish I had known that there would be a chance of our being alone together," the Duke replied, "but unfortunately I have made an appointment to see my Doctor as soon as I return to the Castle and as he is a busy man I really cannot keep him waiting."

"I understand," Jane said, "but it is very, very disappointing and I have so much to talk to you about."

"I know," the Duke agreed, "and I will make sure it will be different when you come to stay at the Castle."

There were two footmen and a Butler waiting at the door to see them off, and the Duke raised Jane's hand to his lips and said:

"Goodbye, Jane. Forgive me for being so remiss at this moment, but it is something I am unable to help."

"I know that," she said, "and I will look forward to Saturday."

The Duke climbed into the pony-cart to pick up the reins with the groom sitting beside him and Ross behind.

As they drove off Jane waved to him and he waved back.

He drove in silence because it was impossible to talk to Ross with the groom present. But when they reached the Castle the Duke walked quickly up the stairs into the Chieftain's Room and Ross followed him.

It was a very impressive room decorated with portraits of the McCarons through the centuries and a large number of stags' antlers.

Ross shut the door and the Duke could hardly wait for the lock to click before he asked:

"Did you find out anything?"

"Yes, Your Grace. They found Miss Giovanna's shoe in the long grass by the drive."

"How do you know that?"

"They asked me, Yer Grace, why when ye left did ye stop in the drive between th' House and th' Lodges."

The Duke stiffened.

"How did they know that?"

"I thinks from what they said that one of the Lodge Keepers was out takin' a stroll, walkin' 'is dog or just being nosey."

"Go on!" the Duke said curtly.

"Anyway, he sees the lights of the carriage stop and they asked me why."

"Who asked you?"

"A strange looking chap, a foreigner."

"A foreigner!" the Duke exclaimed in surprise.

"He weren't in the house when we was, Yer Grace. He came later with that Mr. Horn."

The Duke made no comment and Ross went on:

"When he asks me why we'd stopped, I said that Yer

Grace had felt awful sick and got out of th' carriage rather than mess yerself up inside it.''

The Duke's lips twisted in a faint smile. Ross always had an explanation for everything which invariably amused him.

At the same time there was a worried expression in his eyes.

"What else did he say?"

"Nothing else. It wasn't him that asked me about the shoe, but it had obviously been talked about by everyone in the household. A pretty lass, who I chatted up a bit, said that after we'd left there'd been a real hue an' cry as someone was missing. All they'd been able to find, her giggled, was a shoe—just like Cinderella!''

"The foreigner did not mention it?" the Duke asked.

Ross shook his head.

"No, but I expect he knows. Nasty looking chap. The way he looked at me made I feel that if I said somethin' he didn't like, he'd stick a stiletto into me.''

"Are you saying he is Italian?" the Duke asked.

"He might be, Yer Grace. I could'na be sure. He spoke good English.''

The Duke sighed.

"What we have to do now, Ross," he said after a moment, "is to get Miss Giovanna away.''

"Where to, Yer Grace?"

"That is what I am asking myself,'' the Duke replied.

He left the Chieftain's Room and walked along the passage to see Giovanna.

She was not sitting as he had expected in the armchair that Mrs. Sutherland had arranged for her, but was standing at the open window, looking out at the view.

Mrs. Sutherland was sewing and she rose to her feet as the Duke entered.

"I am back," he said.

Giovanna turned from the window with a cry of delight.

87

"I was not expecting you so soon. Is everything all . . right?"

He knew how important the question was and as Mrs. Sutherland left the room and shut the door behind her, he said:

"Come to sit down, Giovanna. I want to talk to you."

There was a sofa near the fireplace and as she moved towards it he saw she was wearing a blouse made of a blue woollen material and a skirt of the McCaron tartan.

She was still very slender, her waist tiny, and she gave the very ordinary garment that might have been worn by a Highland girl of any class a grace that the Duke thought he might have expected.

She sat down on the sofa, and he realised for the first time that her eyes were very pale green like the waters of a clear stream, flecked with gold.

She looked at him anxiously.

"Something has happened," she said. "You look worried."

"I am only worried because they found one of your shoes."

"How could I have been so stupid as to lose it," Giovanna cried. "Where did they find it?"

"On the drive."

"Now they will know that I did not . . die in the cascade as I . . hoped they would . . think. Did they say anything . . to you?"

"No, it was Ross who found out from one of the housemaids that there had been a commotion because someone was missing."

"I suppose everyone in the House must really have known I was there," Giovanna said as if she spoke to herself.

"How many of them did you see?" the Duke asked.

"Only the old maid who brought up my food . . and

deliberately took it down again, saying I was too . . mad
. . to eat.''

Because she was revealing things the Duke longed to
know, he did not speak. After a moment she went on:

"They all believed I was . . mad, and when at first I
was . . imprisoned in a room on the top floor which was
not in use, I screamed for help.''

As she finished speaking, Giovanna gave a little groan
and put her hands up to her face.

"It is all over now," the Duke said quietly. "You are
safe and all we have to decide is where to take you,
because I think it would be a mistake for you to stay here
much longer.''

She took her hands away from her eyes.

"Yes, of course. You have been so kind, so very kind,
but I do not know where to . . go.''

"I will find somewhere.''

He calculated as he spoke that he had three days to do
so and get Giovanna away before his guests came to stay.

He was sure it had been a wise move to invite them
besides the fact that he was playing for time to avoid
signing the papers that Kane Horn was pressing on him.

"Can you really find somewhere?" Giovanna asked.
"Perhaps it is asking too much and I should go away
on my . . own as I . . suggested.''

"That is something I would certainly not allow you to
do,'' the Duke replied. "Leave everything to me. Just
continue to get stronger and better every day so that you
can begin to enjoy yourself, as you ought to be doing at
your age.''

Giovanna did not answer, but he knew because he
could read her thoughts, that she thought that was
impossible.

He longed to press her to tell him more about herself
and her family, but already his sixth sense was beginning
to tell him what he wanted to know without words.

Yet he wanted to make sure that he was on the right track and not working in the wrong direction. At the same time he had no wish to upset or alarm Giovanna.

She was so fragile, but at the same time so sensitive, that he knew it was more important than anything else, first to get her over the shock of what had occurred.

He must somehow give her a sense of security which would prevent her from believing once again that the only solution to her problem was death.

Aloud he said:

"I want you to trust me, Giovanna, and know that whatever happens I will look after you, and that now there is really no reason for you to be afraid."

She looked up at him and smiled.

"I know why you are saying that, and it is so very kind of you. But you know in your heart that I am . . right to be . . afraid and there is . . nothing else you can do but find me somewhere to hide . . where they will not . . find me."

The Duke had not forgotten that she had said somebody else's life as well as her own was at stake, but he knew he should not try at the moment to persuade her to tell him anymore, and he must be content with what he had already learnt.

Luckily at that moment Ross came into the room with their tea.

There was, as the Duke had predicted, an enormous amount of different homemade delicacies, besides a comb of honey from the hives in the garden and a large heavy fruitcake which he remembered was one of the specialities and regularly baked in the kitchens of the Castle.

He looked in amusement at the laden table and then said:

"Now pour out my tea, and then unless we are to insult the Cook, we have to eat."

"It is impossible for me to eat very much," Giovanna protested.

"You must try," the Duke insisted. "I do not know what you weighed before all this happened to you, but it must have been double or treble what you weigh now!"

She laughed.

"I was never fat! I was what my Nanny used to call 'one of Pharoah's lean kine'."

"Now it is fashionable to be plump," the Duke said, "and every woman wants to be in the fashion."

"Are you saying that is what you like and admire?" Giovanna asked.

It was a question he had never considered before, and the Duke, looking back on the women who had attracted him in India, realised they were on the whole slender with definitely very feminine curves.

That was, however, something he could not say to Giovanna, and he merely replied with a twinkle in his eye:

"As a very busy soldier I have not really had time to notice whether women were fat or thin."

"But you are very insistent that I should be the former!" Giovanna said. "I will try, but I feel it is going to be an impossibility."

"Nothing is impossible," the Duke insisted. "I want you always to remember that, because it is very important that you should really believe that we are going to win the battle, you and I, not only against your being much too thin, but also against all the things that are frightening you."

The way he spoke made Giovanna draw in her breath, and her green, gold-flecked eyes were very large and seemed to fill her whole face as she looked up at him.

Then she said in a voice which was little more than a whisper:

"I do . . believe . . you."

Chapter Five

THE DUKE woke with a strong sense of danger.

It was something which had happened to him several times in India.

Having gone to bed peacefully and without apprehension of anything untoward, he had woken, almost as if someone had touched him with a feeling that something dangerous was imminent, together with a sense of urgency to act.

On each occasion this had happened, his instinct had been correct, and on the last occasion he had saved himself and those he commanded from an unexpected assault which would have annihilated them all.

Now he sat up in bed, realising from the moonlight on either side of the curtains that it was late and he had been asleep for some time.

He got out of bed, went to the nearest window and looked out.

He saw as he expected the Strath lying beneath him, the light from the sky turning the river to silver, and the moors silhouetted darkly against the stars.

The moon was now on the wane and was therefore not

so bright as it had been the night he had found Giovanna beside the cascade.

Yet it was light enough for him to look below and see the garden and terrace of the Castle and to realise at a quick glance there was nothing to perturb him there.

He told himself, as he had done before, that he was imagining the danger he sensed, then he knew that his instinct was stronger than the calculations of his mind, and whether he could see it or not, there was danger.

His thoughts instantly went to Giovanna.

He looked along the side of the Castle, craning forward through the open window to see the protruding walls of the Tower in which she slept.

Then he stiffened and knew that once again his instinct had been right.

There was a definite movement at the foot of the Tower where it was encircled by a balustraded terrace from which a long flight of steps went down into the garden.

It was difficult to see clearly, but he was sure that what he was seeing was two men, perhaps three, dark against the grey stones of the Castle.

He did not waste any more time just looking.

Turning back into his bedroom he picked up his robe from where Ross had left it on a chair, and pulling open the door, began to run speedily down the passage which led to Giovanna's room.

When he reached it he opened the door quietly and saw with a sense of relief she was asleep on the canopied bed.

He could see her clearly, because since she had come to the Castle Mrs. Sutherland had wisely insisted that there should always be a fire burning in her room.

She knew, as the Duke did, that being so emaciated through lack of food Giovanna would feel the cold more acutely than any normal person.

It was actually too early in the year for fires, except

occasionally in the evenings when it was windy or raining.

The Duke had therefore found Giovanna's bedroom when he visited her, almost unpleasantly warm.

Now he was grateful that by the light of the burning logs which were slowly turning to ashes, he could see she had not yet been disturbed.

He shut the door behind him, crossed the room swiftly, and put his hand very gently on her shoulder.

"Wake up," he whispered.

She opened her eyes instantly and he was sure the fear was already in them before he said:

"Get up! You have to hide."

He pulled aside the bedclothes as he spoke and she stepped out of bed in her nightgown. As she did so the Duke pulled the cover which had been folded back on the foot of the mattress, over the bedclothes.

Then he went to the panelled wall behind the bed.

He stood, feeling with his fingers on one of the scrolls which embellished the panelling, and a second later a narrow portion of the wall opened.

The Duke looked round to find Giovanna standing beside him.

Without speaking, he put his arms around her, realising as he did so, she was wearing only a nightgown and the white woollen shawl which Mrs. Sutherland had provided for her shoulders.

He lifted her inside the panel and put her hands on a rung of a ladder which was attached to the wall inside.

"Climb up," he murmured. "I am just behind you."

He closed the panel which led into the bedroom very quietly so that it should not make a noise, and as Giovanna started to climb up the rungs attached to the stone wall he could just discern her small bare feet moving above him.

A little light came from an arrow slit and as he followed Giovanna up to the top of the ladder, they moved into the turret of the Tower which was immediately above her bedroom.

It was not high enough for a man to stand upright, but there was room to sit on the floor without having to crouch down.

The Duke, moving slowly so as not to make any sound, reached the centre of it, and then, feeling with his hand because now there was very little light, he found what he sought.

Slowly he pulled two pieces of wood up from the floor and then reached out to take hold of Giovanna's hand and draw her nearer to him.

Without speaking he put his arm around her and showed her that because he had removed the pieces of wood from the floor they could now look down into the bedroom beneath them.

The peepholes had actually been made hundreds of years earlier and a later Chieftain of the Clan had incorporated them in the plaster design on the ceiling, so that it was impossible to notice them from below.

Looking down, both Giovanna and the Duke could see in the light that came from the fire the centre of the bedroom and would undoubtedly be able to hear anything said in it.

Intent on hiding her, it was only now the Duke was aware how frightened she was.

As he had drawn her close against him to look through the peephole, he could feel her whole body trembling.

He longed to reassure her, but he knew it would be a mistake to speak.

Almost before he expected it, he heard a slight sound that meant someone was climbing up the outside of the Castle to enter the room below them by an open window.

It was not as difficult as it seemed, because the outer surface of the stonework with which the older part of the Castle, especially the towers, had been built was very uneven, many of the stones protruding and sadly in need of pointing which the late Duke had not been able to afford.

Talbot as a boy had often with his cousins climbed up the outside of the Castle, even though they were forbidden to do so.

The turret in which he and Giovanna were now hiding was one of their favourite places where they could escape from their Tutor and others who were engaged to look after them.

His elder cousin had always boasted to his younger brother and to Talbot that he in fact was the only person who was supposed to know the secrets of the various hiding-places in the Castle.

"It is something which is handed down from each Chieftain to his eldest son," he had said, "and you are not to tell Papa that you have been here with me!"

"No, of course not!" his brother and Talbot had promised.

But Talbot had found it thrilling to know that there were secret hiding-places where a fugitive could escape from those who pursued him, and if enemies actually penetrated into the Castle, the Chieftain and his family could save themselves from being taken prisoner.

Now he knew it must have been his instinct that had made him take Giovanna to the turret of the Tower rather than to one of the other bedrooms which were larger and more comfortable.

He was not certain for a moment whether the sounds he heard came from outside and were relayed through the air holes which were hidden under the ledge of the roof or whether the men who were searching for Giovanna were already inside her bedroom.

Then they could see through the peepholes a dark figure appear in the centre of the floor and a man said in a low voice:

"She's not here."

"Gone!" another voice exclaimed.

Just that single word told the Duke that it was Kane Horn who spoke.

He had a fleeting glimpse of him moving below as he stood looking at the bed and said:

"You told me she was here this morning!"

"She were, Sir, I see'd her with me own eyes standin' at th' window."

"Then he must have got her away unless she's in another room."

Kane Horn moved again so that both Giovanna and the Duke could see the top of his head beneath them.

He stood still as if he was thinking, and then said sharply:

"Look into the other rooms, but be careful not to wake anyone. If there's a fire here in this room, she's likely to have a fire anywhere else she's sleeping."

It sounded logical and the man to whom he was speaking must have gone from the room without a reply, for Kane Horn said no more nor did he move from where he was standing.

Then a few seconds later as if he could not bear the inaction, he followed the man who had left him.

But the Duke thought that he would in fact, only go into the passage and would not actually search himself in case he was seen.

It was just an idea, but as the space beneath them cleared Giovanna looked up at him and he knew she was going to say something.

Because he knew it was dangerous, the Duke without thinking acted instantaneously and silenced her lips with his.

His mouth came down on hers, and at the same time he pulled her closer fearing lest by one unwary word they would reveal their hiding-place.

He felt her stiffen with surprise.

Then as his lips held hers captive he was aware not only that he was kissing her but the softness of her mouth, the quivering of her body, and the helpless little movement she made with her hands, gave him a strange feeling he had never known before.

It was something he could not explain even to himself.

Yet he felt as if the vibrations which had drawn him to Giovanna in the first place now joined them indivisibly.

They had made him aware of what she had been about to do at the cascade and had forced him against his better judgement to save her not only from herself but from the people of whom she was afraid.

Now the same vibrations became intensified until his lips told him that Giovanna belonged to him.

He could not explain, he only knew that as his mouth became more possessive her lips gave him a rapture he had never experienced in the whole of his life.

He knew too, without being told that the terror which had made her tremble had now become a quiver of ecstasy which made her forget that she was afraid or that she was being hunted.

Just for one second the Duke released Giovanna's lips to draw in his breath, and then he was kissing her again, kissing her with a long slow demanding kiss which made her pulsate to him until he could feel thrills like shafts of lightning moving through them both.

Without realising what he was doing, he pulled his robe open, so that her body could be closer to his.

There were now only two pieces of silk between them, and the closeness of it was part of the same glory as their kisses.

Then suddenly, when it seemed to the Duke that with Giovanna he was touching the stars, a voice, not loud but hard and sharp, broke in on them, and they came back to earth.

"You've found nothing?"

It was Kane Horn who asked the question and the Duke knew he had been right in guessing he had not gone far from the open door.

Now he moved back into the room followed by the man who had gone to search for Giovanna.

"Nothin' Sir. The rooms are all closed an' empty except for one."

"Which one?"

"I think it's the Master's Room. The bed has been slept in, but there was no-one there."

The Duke knew he was speaking of his room and there was silence until Kane Horn said:

"They must have gone away. Who else was watching the house besides you?"

"Only Antonio, and he ain't much of a hand with a spyglass. Shall I ask him what he saw?"

The man speaking was moving towards the window when Kane Horn said sharply:

"No, you fool! If they have gone, the Duke will have taken her to a railway station from where she can travel home."

"Home? Do yer mean to Italy?"

"Of course I mean Naples! Where else would she go?"

There was a short silence before Kane Horn said harshly:

"By letting her get away you've mucked it up between you, but it's of no account. We can kill her there more easily than we can here, and the old woman with her."

"You should have done that when she arrived as I says at the time."

"I know, I know!" Kane Horn said irritably. "But it might have been more difficult in Scotland with too many people to ask questions."

"Well, what are we going to do now?" the man asked.

"I've told you. We leave for Italy and make no mistakes this time!"

"That sounds more like you. Now how do we get out of this old ruin?"

"Through a door!" Kane Horn said sharply. "There'll be one which leads into the garden, and you can collect Antonio."

He walked across the bedroom as he spoke and the Duke saw the head of the other man following him.

They did not close the door, but their feet made no sound moving down the corridor.

The Duke however, sat very still for a long time, holding Giovanna against him and putting his finger to her lips just in case she spoke.

He was too experienced not to know that it was always dangerous to assume a room was empty.

Then at last when he thought it was safe, he took his finger from Giovanna's lips and putting his hand under her chin, turned her face up to his.

He would have kissed her, but she made a sound like a small animal in pain and turned her head so that she could hide it against his neck.

"It is all right, my darling," the Duke said. "I will not let them kill you, you know that."

"But they . . will kill . . Grandmama, because they are . . afraid she would . . identify me."

"As I have already done. Why did you not trust me?"

"I was so afraid . . so desperately . . afraid because my Stepmother said if I ever . . betrayed them in . . any way, she would not only . . kill me but . . Grandmama as . . well."

Her words were almost incoherent with tears and the Duke held her very closely against him, his lips on her hair.

"Now we have to move very quickly," he said.

"What . . do we . . do?" Giovanna asked with a sob.

"We are leaving at once for Italy," he said, "to save your Grandmother and you from these fiends."

He gave a sigh before he said:

"At least now there need be no more secrets between us. But we have no time to do anything but leave as they think we have already done."

He moved ahead of Giovanna, climbing down the secret stairway and opened the panel into the bedroom so she could see her way more clearly.

At the same time he helped her, putting each of her small, naked feet on the rungs of the ladder until as she stood beside him he held her against him and kissed her gently.

"I love you," he said, "and love is stronger than evil and invincible even against the most unpleasant thugs I have ever encountered."

"Can you . . really save . . Grandmama?"

She spoke in little gasps and the Duke knew it was because she was pulsating from his kiss, and in the light from the fire he could see that her eyes were shining and seemed to fill her whole face.

He took her back into the bedroom and pulling open the bed, lifted her into it.

"Now stay there and rest," he ordered, "while I set the wheels rolling. As you are well aware, they have to roll very quickly."

Giovanna looked at him and there were no words to express what she was feeling.

He wanted to kiss her to reassure her that they would win, but he knew time was important and without saying anything more, he went from the room to ring the bell for Ross and start dressing.

Because both the Duke and Ross were used to emergencies in which a few seconds could mean the difference between life and death, they actually drove away from the Castle only an hour and a half later.

Mrs. Sutherland had produced some clothes for Giovanna to wear which the Duke knew had belonged to his Aunt.

She had fortunately been a small woman and, although the clothes were simple and only suitable to be worn in Scotland, the Duke knew it was of primary importance that Giovanna should be clothed somehow.

What Mrs. Sutherland did produce in case she was cold, was a slightly old-fashioned but very beautiful Sable fur coat which the Duke's Aunt had worn the last years of her life.

It was, he thought, a very sensible garment which would protect Giovanna from the cold.

He thought too he could wrap her in it so that she could sleep as much as possible on what was going to be a very arduous journey, even for someone in good health.

Ross was of course invaluable, and it was he who alerted the coachman and got the travelling-carriage drawn by four horses ready in record time.

It was the Duke who suggested they should leave from the Stables rather than the front door, just in case Kane Horn's men were still watching the Castle, even though he thought it unlikely.

Actually he was certain that by whatever means they had arrived from Dalbeth House, they would now have returned, and would be making their plans to leave, as they were, for Italy.

Whatever way they travelled, whether by sea or by road to the nearest railway station, he and Giovanna must get ahead of them.

He knew now he had been right in thinking that Kane Horn was Italian.

He may have been living in America, but it was obvious from what he said, that his home was in Italy, doubtless in Naples itself.

The Dowager Countess would have told him of the immense fortune Jane had inherited but he might have also heard it talked about and exclaimed over locally.

There was a great deal the Duke wanted to know and

102

to understand, and some of his questions would obviously be answered when he could talk to Giovanna.

However for the moment all that mattered was speed.

He had to make arrangements to see that he had enough money for the journey, and also to make some explanation to the Clan.

Hastily, while Ross was packing, he sat down at his desk and wrote to Sir Iain McCaron.

He told him that he had been sent for by the Secretary of State for India, to give an account of what had happened on the North-West Frontier just before he came home.

"You will understand," he wrote in a neat upright hand, *"that it is a request I cannot refuse as officially I am still a Serving Officer. I will however return as soon as I possibly can, but as I know you are aware, these enquiries, which incidentally are Top-Secret, often take a long time. Will you therefore make my apologies to the Dowager Countess whom I invited to stay this coming weekend and also her Stepdaughter? Tell the Elders of the Clan that I am in my absence leaving everything in your hands. Go ahead with the repairs that are of immediate importance, and I enclose a cheque for the wages and any urgent demands that have to be met before my return."*

He then wrote a cheque which he knew would, together with the money he required for the journey, use up his entire bank balance, and leave him in debt for the future, but it seemed of little importance.

It was not money that worried him at that moment, but lives, the most important being Giovanna's.

He finished his letter to Sir Iain and as he sealed it he thought not only was he engaged in one of the most dangerous exploits he had ever undertaken, he had also, although he could hardly believe it himself, fallen wildly and head-over-heels in love.

It seemed impossible that it should have happened so quickly.

Yet his instinct, which he never denied, told him that what he was feeling now was not only different from anything he had ever felt before for a woman, but was something so fundamentally wonderful that it marked the beginning of a new life that he had never dreamt of or expected.

Carrying the letter to Sir Iain in his hand, he went from his desk to find, as he expected, the Steward in charge of the household waiting for him outside.

"Oi understands Yer Grace has to go South," the old man remarked.

He was obviously a trifle bemused at being woken so hastily in the middle of the night.

"It is something I have to do, Donald," the Duke replied. "I know you will look after everything while I am away. What is important is that I want nobody outside the Castle itself to know that we left during the night. Instead, if you are asked, will you say I drove away late in the afternoon."

The Steward looked surprised, but he replied stolidly:

"Ye can rely on me to say what Yer Grace wishes."

"Thank you, Donald, and the less it is talked about the better. Of course, as Mrs. Sutherland will tell you, no-one except those you can trust, must be aware that there was a young lady with me."

"Oi'll see to it, Yer Grace."

The Duke did not say anymore, but quickly ran down some stairs and along a passage which carried him through a side door which led directly to the Stables.

The carriage was ready and he found Ross and Mrs. Sutherland had already taken Giovanna downstairs and she was waiting for him in the carriage.

He thought as he looked at her in the light of the stable-lamps that she looked very lovely enveloped in his

Aunt's Sable coat and with a little Sable-trimmed bonnet on her fair hair.

"Now ye take care of yerself," Mrs. Sutherland was saying, "and drink yer milk at least three times a day. Promise me."

"I will do my best," Giovanna answered. "And thank you, dear Mrs. Sutherland, for being so kind."

There was a little sob in her voice as she spoke, and the Duke had the feeling that she was afraid that she was saying goodbye, not only to Mrs. Sutherland but to the Castle.

He touched Mrs. Sutherland on the shoulder as he climbed into the carriage.

Then as the wheels started to move he knew Ross had jumped up on the box and the luggage they were taking with them was already on top of the carriage and strapped on behind.

He took Giovanna's hand in his and said:

"Now we are off on the last lap of our adventure, and as we are going together I hope you think it is rather exciting."

She turned her face towards him.

As it was not yet dawn, although the moonlight and stars were fading from the sky, he could not see the expression in her eyes.

But there was a little catch in her voice as she asked:

"You . . are not angry . . with me . . for not . . telling you who . . I was?"

"I wish you had trusted me," the Duke answered, "but at the same time I guessed."

"How could you . . have guessed?"

"I think the most convincing thing was that you kept your own name."

He felt her fingers stiffen in surprise before she asked:

"You knew Giovanna meant 'Jane' in Italian?"

"I am not entirely an ignoramus!"

"No, of course not," she replied, "but few people would have known, and I told Papa in a letter that it was what the girls called me at the Convent."

"So your Stepmother told you your name was to be Giovanna."

"Yes."

He felt a little shiver go through her as she spoke of her Stepmother, and he said quickly:

"We are not going to talk about it now because there is a long journey in front of us. It is a story I want you to tell me to pass away the hours, but which I do not want to upset you."

"How can I . . help being . . upset when I have . . involved you in . . something so . . terrible."

"I think you know I love you and I would loathe and detest not being involved in anything which concerns you."

He felt her fingers cling to his as she said:

"Only you would say . . something so . . wonderful, and if you . . love me . . I have loved you from the very first moment I looked at you after you had . . taken me away from the . . cascade."

"We are not going to talk about the cascade," the Duke said, "for the simple reason it frightens me to think that I might have lost you. All I want to talk about now is our love and to tell you that I have been looking for you all my life. But I had become convinced that you did not exist, when suddenly, like a miracle, you are here!"

He paused for a moment before he said, his voice very deep:

"You are mine, Giovanna, and I will never lose you!"

Chapter Six

As the French train left Calais the Duke heaved a sigh of relief.

At the same time he could not help feeling a little amused that in his new position life was smoothed for him in a manner he could hardly have believed possible.

When they reached Inverness Station he had sent a number of telegrams from the Station Master's Office asking for a Courier to meet him in London, and for arrangements to be made for his journey to Naples.

The Station Master was obviously impressed with the importance of the Duke of Invercaron.

When he and Giovanna were escorted by several Officials into two reserved sleeping-compartments with Ross in an adjoining compartment, he thought it was very different from the way he had had to scramble for a seat in the past.

Giovanna was already tired, and the Duke had a sleeping-berth made up and insisted on her lying down.

She had as he knew, been nervous that something might happen to her on the journey, and although he had promised it was perfectly safe once the train was moving, he realised that when night came she would be terrified alone in the dark.

He was also half-afraid that by some unfortunate coincidence Kane Horn might get on the same train.

He therefore had the second bunk in Giovanna's compartment made up and he lay on it without undressing.

He knew that because he was with her for the first time since leaving the Castle she fell into a deep sleep.

He was sure that because she loved him she would not be so agitated as she would have been otherwise.

He was certain of this when they sat talking together in a private cabin while they crossed the Channel.

He was half-afraid that she would be upset by the sea, but he had the feeling, although he did not mention it, that because she was so happy to be with him and to know that he loved her she was hardly aware of anything else.

The Courier who had been engaged for him by the Railway Authorities at St. Pancras, was a competent man who spoke, he assured the Duke, both French and Italian.

As soon as he understood exactly what was required he sent urgent telegrams to all the necessary authorities, with the result that not only did they have a private cabin on the ship, but also, which the Duke had never enjoyed before, a private coach attached to the Express waiting at Calais.

Giovanna was delighted.

"I have always heard that the Queen travels like this," she said, "but now I know that a Duke is just as Royal!"

The Duke laughed.

"Not exactly," he said, "but I am pleased that you will be more comfortable than you might otherwise have been."

Their coach was very luxurious and there were two

sleeping-compartments with brass bedsteads in them and everything else fitted to the walls.

"It is like having a little house all to ourselves," Giovanna exclaimed.

"That is what we will have very soon," the Duke said quietly.

She looked up at him and he saw the happiness in her eyes which was then replaced by an expression of apprehension concerning what lay ahead.

The Duke took off her bonnet in which she had travelled and unbuttoned her coat, but he did not remove it in case she should feel cold.

"Come and sit down," he said. "As soon as the train starts Ross is going to serve us with dinner which I ordered ahead, and I think we both need a glass of champagne."

"All I want is that the train should go very, very quickly," Giovanna replied.

The Duke knew she was frantic in case Kane Horn should arrive in Naples before they did.

To reassure her he said:

"I am prepared to bet a large sum of money, which I do not possess, that we are way ahead of our enemies and remember they will not have the same 'Royal' facilities as we have."

He thought she was reassured, and knew it would be a mistake to go on talking of what lay in the future, about which he in fact, was extremely apprehensive.

On his instructions the Courier had already sent telegrams to the Chief of Police in Naples, but knowing how indolent the Italians could sometimes be the Duke wondered if his title would carry as much weight in a foreign country as it did in England.

He was also worried about Giovanna in case she should collapse on such an arduous journey being still so weak.

There was however nothing he could do about that except cosset her in every way he could, and Ross was even more insistent than he was that she should rest.

They ate a delicious meal provided, the Duke was aware, by the best hotel in Calais, which therefore cost a considerable sum of money.

When it was finished Ross said:

"Now come along, Miss. Ye know what Mrs. Sutherland'd say if she was with us, that ye mustna dare open yer eyes until it's daylight."

Giovanna laughed and the Duke thought it was a very pretty sound.

"I think you are bullying me," she protested, "but I admit I am actually very tired."

Ross went ahead to open the door which led into her bedroom and she looked at the Duke.

"I will come and kiss you goodnight," he said, "but now you must do as Ross says."

She gave him a little smile and walked slowly, holding onto the chairs as she passed them, through the open door.

After a short while Ross came back.

"Now dinna ye worry, Yer Grace," he said. "Her Ladyship'll be all right."

It was the first time he had referred to her in her rightful style, and the Duke looked at him reflectively before he asked:

"You are aware, Ross, who Miss Giovanna really is?"

"I had ma suspicions, Yer Grace, from the very beginning," Ross replied, "but I didna want tae have ma head snapped off, if I suggested it tae ye."

The Duke smiled and asked:

"What made you suspicious?"

"The way that young woman at Dalbeth House looked the first night we dined there," Ross answered. "I saw her coming down tae dinner after ye went into the

Drawing-Room, an' I said to meself: 'She's na a Scot, or I'll eat me bonnet!' "

"That was very clever of you," the Duke said. "I did not at that time, suspect she was an imposter, but merely over-sophisticated and over-painted in a way that would certainly shock our Clansmen."

"Her shocked the Macbeths right enough," Ross said. "Ye shoulda heard what they said aboot her in the Servants' Hall!"

The Duke could imagine how horrified the old servants would have been that any girl so young and also their Chieftain should be powdered and painted in a manner they would have expected of a harlot.

"I saw th' men, Yer Grace," Ross said as he took the glasses from the table, "an' we'll have to have our wits aboot us tae cope wi' them."

"I know that," the Duke agreed quietly, "but whatever happens we must avoid upsetting Lady Sinclair who, I understand, is in very delicate health."

He knew by the expression on Ross's face that he thought this might be an impossibility, but he did not say anything before retiring to the small kitchen which lay at the other end of the coach.

There was a folding bed in it and the Duke was glad that Ross was near him and did not, as often happened, have to get off at the first stop in order to transfer to one of the ordinary carriages.

The Courier, however, had been clever enough to ensure that they were attached to an Express and there was actually only one stop between Calais and Paris.

They reached there early in the morning. Although the Duke was up and dressed he did not disturb Giovanna, and when later he peeped into her compartment she was still asleep.

She had in fact been almost asleep when he went as he had promised to say goodnight to her.

111

He had therefore only kissed her very gently.

Because she was looking so lovely with her fair hair falling over the pillow he longed to stay talking to her and kissing her.

But he knew she was completely exhausted, and almost before he left her eyes were closed and she was drifting away into unconsciousness.

It was the best thing that could happen, and yet when the Duke went back to the Drawing-Room he was aware that the blood was throbbing in his temples because he had touched her and his heart was behaving in an unpredictable manner.

"How is it possible," he asked himself, "that at my age and with all my long experience I should feel like a boy with his first love?"

It seemed incredible, and yet he knew the Indians believed that the real love which came from Krishna was Divine, and of those who sought it most were disappointed.

The Duke knew that he had now found the love that was his by the Wheel of Rebirth although it had never struck him that somebody like Giovanna was waiting for him if he could only find her.

A streak of fear shot through him at the thought that if he had reached the cascade even a few seconds later than he had, he would have been too late and would never have known she existed.

But he had not been too late.

He had found her and now like one of the heroes of mythology he had to rescue her not from Demons or Dragons but from a gang of unscrupulous avaricious criminals who were prepared to kill for money.

There was so much he wanted to know about them which only Giovanna could tell him but he must wait until she was prepared to talk.

It was not until some time after they had left Paris and

were speeding South that she came into the Drawing-Room, looking so lovely after her night's rest that the Duke gave an exclamation of joy at seeing her.

"I am ashamed of having slept for so long," she said as he put out his hand to help her into a comfortable armchair by the window.

"It was the most sensible thing you could do," he said.

"When Ross brought me my breakfast at 10 o'clock, I could hardly believe I had slept right through the night."

"You did not feel afraid?" the Duke asked.

"I knew that . . you were near me and that . . you were . . protecting me."

The way she spoke was very touching and he said:

"Shall I tell you how lovely you look, or do you feel it is too early in the day to talk of anything so exciting?"

She laughed.

"I want to think I look lovely for you, but I am very conscious of how my bones are sticking out and of the lines on my face."

"Do not worry about that," the Duke said. "In a few days, especially in the sunshine, you will look as you did before you came to Scotland."

"I hope . . so," Giovanna said in a low voice.

Ross interrupted by bringing them a pot of steaming coffee with some fresh cream which he had taken on board at Paris.

There was also a jug of milk for Giovanna and when she saw it she exclaimed:

"Please . . may I have some coffee with it? Mrs. Sutherland made me drink so much milk that I am afraid I shall turn into a cow!"

The Duke laughed.

"I think that is unlikely, but you will find it will taste nicer if you mix it with coffee, we will do that until we return home."

She gave him a quick glance which he knew meant that

113

she was praying fervently that she would be allowed to return home with him.

He therefore said quietly when Ross had left them alone:

"Drink your coffee, then I want you to help me make plans. But it will be difficult unless I know exactly what has been happening and why you went to Naples in the first place."

Giovanna gave a deep sigh, then she slipped her hand in his in a confiding, child-like manner which the Duke found very touching.

He kissed her fingers one by one until she said:

"If you do that . . I will find it . . difficult to think of anything but . . you."

"Just as I can only think that you are the most perfect, adorable person I have ever met in my life," the Duke said in a deep voice.

"Is that . . true?"

He looked at her for a long moment before he said:

"Before we start talking about what has happened to you, my darling, before we even mention the future, I want to tell you one thing."

He felt her fingers tremble as if she was afraid, and he said:

"Look at me!"

She turned her head and he thought her gold-flecked eyes, even with a very worried expression in them, were the most beautiful things he had ever seen.

"What I am going to say," he said in a deep voice, "is that if you were not who you are, if you were someone quite different, without a single penny to your name, I would still go down on my knees and beg you to be my wife."

As he spoke he knew it was something she had not expected him to say.

Then suddenly her face was radiant and her fingers tightened on his.

114

She did not speak, but her lips parted as if she found it hard to breathe.

"Do you believe me?" the Duke asked. "For I swear by Almighty God that is the truth."

"I do believe you," Giovanna answered, "but it is my horrible . . money which has . . been the cause of . . everything that has . . happened to me! I only wish my Godmother had left it to . . somebody else!"

It was a cry that came from her heart and the Duke said quietly:

"I knew that you would feel like that! At the same time, my precious, you know what it will mean to your people as well as mine, who are so desperately in need of help."

"Will you promise to look after them . . first?" she asked.

The Duke smiled.

"That is what I would have expected you to say, and I was only afraid that the Countess of Dalbeth would be more concerned with new gowns than leaking roofs, and perhaps would find London more exciting than a crumbling Castle!"

"How can you imagine I could ever . . . ?" Giovanna began.

Then she realised that the Duke was only teasing her.

"I used to worry about the Clansmen when I was in Naples," she said, "and I knew without being told that Stepmama was spending all Papa's money on herself and leaving nothing for the crofters and those in the Glen who were always desperately poor."

"How could your father have married anybody so utterly unworthy?" the Duke asked.

"*She* married him!" Giovanna replied.

The Duke remembered how Sir Iain McCaron had said much the same thing, and he asked:

"Now tell me what happened."

"Papa went to Edinburgh to stay with some friends for a Regimental dinner that was being given at the Castle. I was glad he was going because he had been so unhappy after . . Mama died and sometimes I . . I thought that without her he had . . lost the . . will to . . live."

There was a little sob in Giovanna's voice, and the Duke knew how unhappy she had been at the time.

"He was away for longer than I had expected," she continued, "and when he returned . . *she* was . . with him!"

"They were married?"

"They told me they had been married very quietly . . although Papa could remember nothing about it."

The Duke stared at Giovanna in astonishment.

"Did he really say that?"

"I was sure later that my Stepmother had drugged him by putting something in his wine which made him do exactly what she wanted . . of which afterwards, he had no recollection."

The way she spoke made the Duke ask:

"What made you certain that was what she had done?"

"Because it was what she did after they . . returned whenever she wanted something . . special from . . him."

"Tell me exactly what happened then," the Duke begged.

"From the moment they came home Papa started to drink a great deal more than he had ever done before. It was not just an occasional whisky which he had always enjoyed, but bottles of claret and port, and champagne which she preferred."

"Did you speak to him about it?" the Duke asked.

"Of course I did," Giovanna answered. "I said:

" 'Please, Papa, do not drink so much. You know it would upset Mama if she were here, and it makes me embarrassed and unhappy when you are not really yourself.' ''

"What did your father reply to that?"

"The first time I spoke to him he said:

" 'You are quite right, my dearest, and I know I am making a fool of myself. I promise to be more sensible from now on.' ''

"And was he?"

"He tried . . I know he tried!" Giovanna said earnestly, "but my Stepmother was furious with me."

"What did she say?"

"She told me to mind my own business and that she would look after my father, and she knew what was best for him."

"So he went on drinking."

"He tried not to do so in front of me, but I realised that whenever my Stepmother wanted him to give her some money she would take him a glass of claret or port, and say:

" 'I have brought you a drink, dearest Ewan, and I want you to drink a toast with me because we are so happy together.' ''

Giovanna paused and the Duke asked:

"What happened then?"

"I realised after this had happened two or three times that my Stepmother must be putting something very potent into his glass, because immediately Papa had drunk it he became almost insensible, or what appeared to be very, very drunk."

The Duke's lips tightened before he asked:

"Did you accuse your Stepmother of doing anything like that?"

"I accused her of many things," Giovanna replied, "but most of all of spending money which we could not afford. After Mama died I would help Papa with the accounts, and I knew that before he married my Step-

117

mother we had economised very strictly in order to help the Clansmen, many of whom are on the verge of starvation.''

She drew in her breath as if she was remembering how upsetting it was and went on:

"When the winter had been hard they had nothing to eat, it was pitiful," she continued. "Always in the past when this happened Papa and Mama used to help them over the bad times."

"Of course," the Duke murmured, knowing it was what every decent Chieftain did.

"But when they came as they always had to the house for help," Giovanna went on, "my Stepmother sent them away, telling them that my father was too ill to be worried with their complaints."

She gave a deep sigh.

"I knew how wrong and wicked that was when Papa was their Chieftain, and if he had been himself, he would never have let them be treated in such a callous manner."

"What did you do?"

"I gave when I could, any money that was available and spoke to one of the Elders of the Clan who provided the small children with milk which had always been Papa's responsibility."

Giovanna looked away from the Duke as if she was embarrassed as she said:

"What was so degrading was that my Stepmother was buying new curtains, new carpets, and expensive ornaments for the house and decorating it in a most extravagant manner while our people were . . hungry."

As if she could not help it her voice broke and the tears ran down her cheeks.

The Duke put his arm around her shoulders.

"If this is upsetting you too much, my precious," he said, "we will talk about it another time."

He wiped away her tears, then Giovanna said:

"No . . I want to go on . . I want you to know . . It is so . . wonderful to be able to talk to you . . when I thought that nobody would . . ever again understand . . and I should . . die with the secrets . . inside me."

"Your secrets now are mine, as mine are yours," the Duke said, "but you must tell me your story another time."

"No . . now!" Giovanna replied almost fiercely.

He kissed her forehead, then sat back again in his own chair, still holding her hand.

As he did so an idea came to him and he said:

"As you are so regrettably thin, I believe there is room for us together and if you are going to go on with your story I want to hold you closer than I can at the moment."

He had been right.

When he had seated himself beside her there was still room, if he held her close to him.

She made a little sound of contentment and put her head on his shoulder and the Duke said:

"Now I think it will be easier and a great deal more pleasant because I can feel you against my heart."

"I . . like being . . close to you," Giovanna murmured.

She looked up at him and the Duke wanted to kiss her, but he thought it would interrupt what it was imperative he should know and he therefore said:

"Go on with what you were telling me."

"It was then . . after I had fought with her about the Clansmen, and told her we could not afford the money she was spending, that my Stepmother showed me how much she . . hated me."

She gave a little shiver before she said:

"I could feel her hatred pouring out from her almost as if it was something . . alive . . and very evil."

"Which it was!" the Duke murmured thinking of what had happened afterwards.

119

"Everything I did, everything I said was wrong," Giovanna went on, "and finally I suggested to Papa that I should go away."

"Did he understand?"

"He said:

" 'Your Stepmother has been suggesting for some time that you should go to a Boarding School.' "

"Were you surprised?"

"No . . I was only afraid that she would . . choose the School."

"So you went to stay with your grandmother."

"I had received a letter from her asking how I was and when I showed it to Papa he said:

" 'Why do you not go and stay in Naples? I think you would be happier there.' "

"Were you surprised at the idea?" the Duke asked.

"At first. It had never struck me that I might leave Scotland. Then I looked at Papa and realised how much he had deteriorated."

She sighed and went on:

"We were talking early in the morning before Stepmother was awake. He had had too much to drink the night before, and I knew that if she was aware I was with him and we were happy together, she would bring him one of her poisonous glasses of wine. Then he would become so drunk that I would not be able to talk to him."

Giovanna was silent for a moment before she said very touchingly:

"I felt as if . . Mama was beside me . . telling me what to say and . . I asked Papa if I should write to my grandmother and suggest that I visit her."

"And he agreed?"

"He urged me not only to write, but to go at once! I think . . at that moment he was aware not only of how much I was suffering . . but that he was suffering himself from the woman who was destroying him . . but about whom he could . . do nothing!''

There was so much unhappiness in Giovanna's voice that the Duke held her even closer to him, and put his lips against the softness of her cheek.

"It must have been very hard for you, my darling."

"P . perhaps I was . . wrong and should have . . stayed," Giovanna said, "but because it was all so . . horrible and so unlike the happiness we had known with Mama . . I wanted almost frantically to get away."

"I can understand that. After all, you were only fifteen."

"I was old enough to realise how terrible it all was, but not old enough to save . . Papa."

The Duke was aware that as a young and inexperienced girl there was nothing she could have done against a woman as dangerous as her Stepmother.

"So you left for Naples?" he asked.

"Colonel Dalbeth, who was Papa's cousin, sent his daughter who was a very sensible woman of over thirty-five to escort me there. We did not travel grandly like you, but Second-Class, but it was all rather fun and an adventure."

"Your grandmother was pleased to see you?"

"Delighted, but I thought it was somehow wrong to leave Papa . . and I meant to go back soon."

"Do you suppose he would have let you?"

"I wrote to Papa every week and he answered once or twice . . then when I wrote and asked if he wanted me to come home, my Stepmother replied."

"I can guess what she said!" the Duke remarked.

"She made it very clear that neither she nor my father wished to see me. I was to stay where I was and not have any stupid ideas about returning to Scotland."

"Then what happened?"

"Grandmama had already arranged for me to have

121

some lessons from various teachers, but when she knew I was staying for good she thought it would be best if I became a boarder at the Convent School, as I would have girls there of my own age to talk to, and also have better teachers than those I was having at the moment.''

"So you went to live at the Convent," the Duke said. "It seems strange, in a way."

"It was very different from what I had imagined a Convent would be," Giovanna answered. "On one side were the dedicated Sisters who prayed all the time or attended to the very poor in Naples."

"You were not allowed to be with them?" the Duke asked.

"No," Giovanna replied. "On the other side was the School which was attended by thirty pupils, all of whom came from the best families in Italy or France. We had highly experienced teachers in all subjects, but they were not always Nuns."

She smiled.

"Although we had to attend a lot of Services and had hours of religious teaching every week, we were also extremely well taught on other subjects."

Giovanna paused before she looked up at the Duke and said:

"I am so very glad now that I . . learnt so much . . because otherwise . . you would find me very ignorant . . and perhaps be . . bored with me."

"I could never be that!" the Duke said.

"But I am afraid my learning is all from books, whereas you have travelled about the world, fought in India and been very, very brave."

The Duke laughed.

"You have been listening to Mrs. Sutherland and Ross, and when you know me well you may find me very different from their picture of me."

"I know you well . . enough to know that . . you are

very . . wonderful!'' Giovanna said in a soft, shy voice.

Then as the Duke did not speak she added quickly:

"You do love me . . you do really love me . . you are not just saying it . . to make me happy?''

"I love you as I have never loved anyone in my whole life,'' the Duke answered. "In fact, I had no idea I could feel as I feel about you, my lovely one.''

"You . . you are . . sure of that?''

"Absolutely sure,'' he said, "and it is something I will prove to you as soon as you are safe and we are married.''

As he spoke he turned her face up to his and kissed her. As he felt their vibrations join and they became one person he knew, that there was really no need for words.

He kissed Giovanna until her eyes were shining like the sunshine outside, and he knew she was feeling the same ecstasy that he was feeling himself.

"I love you—God, how I love you!'' he exclaimed. "I wish we could go away together on a honeymoon, my darling, and forget everything but ourselves.''

But as he spoke he knew that the dark menacing hand of Kane Horn overshadowed them both.

He told himself the sooner it was brought into the open and finished once and for all the better.

All he could do at the moment was to think of Giovanna and kiss her until everything except the wonder of their love was, for the moment, forgotten.

*　　　*　　　*

It was much later in the day after Giovanna had slept for a long time after an excellent luncheon before they could continue their conversation.

She had come back into the Drawing-Room where the Duke was waiting for her, and was wearing a pretty gown of a soft blue material which he knew must have belonged to his Aunt.

Mrs. Sutherland had altered it to fit Giovanna, and while it was not a very elaborate gown it was swept back into some semblance of a fashionable bustle.

Its very simplicity made Giovanna look sylph-like, and as he had first thought her to be, a nymph from the cascade.

The pale gold of her hair, the green of her eyes, and the dazzling whiteness of her skin gave her the look of an Immortal while the slenderness of her body made her ethereal and insubstantial.

The Duke drew her down to the end of the carriage where there was a seat from which during her absence he had had an arm of the chair removed and thereby created what was in fact, a small sofa.

"As I like you close to me," he said, "I think we shall be more comfortable here than in one armchair."

Giovanna smiled.

"I was very comfortable as we were . . but as long as I can still be . . near to you . . I do not mind where we are."

"As that is what I want too," the Duke replied, "we are in complete agreement, my lovely!"

He kissed her gently and touched the silkiness of her hair with his hand.

"How can you manage to look so beautiful after all you have been through?" he asked.

"That is what I wanted you to say. At the same time, I think you must be blind," Giovanna replied. "I am very ashamed of my looks, and to please you and Mrs. Sutherland I have drunk all the milk that Ross brought me at the last place where we stopped."

She wrinkled her small nose and added:

"I do not think French milk is very nice!"

"We will think of something else to fatten you up," the Duke promised.

"I think being happy with you is better for me than anything I could eat," Giovanna whispered.

Because it was what he thought himself he kissed her.

It was quite a long time before Giovanna returned, because she knew it was something she must do, to where her story had been interrupted.

"It was in May that I had a letter from Scotland telling me that Papa . . was dead."

"Was it a terrible shock?"

"It was what I expected because I had not heard from him for such a long time. I always wrote to him . . but he never replied . . and I had a feeling, perhaps because I am 'fey' that it would not be long before he . . joined Mama . . in Heaven."

She spoke very simply but the Duke new that she regretted that her father had died without her being there to say goodbye to him and instead had left him at the mercy of a woman who hated her.

"And when did you let them know you would go back?"

"I did not think of that at first . . but then I had a letter from Colonel Macbeth and other members of the Clan to say I must return as I was now the Countess of Dalbeth and hereditary Chieftain."

She paused as if she was remembering how upsetting it had been.

"They did however suggest," she went on, "that if I was at School I might wish to finish the term."

"Was that what you wanted?"

"Yes, of course, I was so nervous of going back to Scotland. Grandmama and I discussed it together and thought it most important that I should pass my examinations which all came at the end of the summer term."

"Then what happened?"

"A letter suddenly arrived from America to say that my Godmother was dead and she had left me a fortune!"

"It must have been a great surprise!"

"It was! At the same time I realised I could now help the Macbeths and the other Clansmen about whom I had worried all the time, knowing that when I was not there Stepmother would just send them away empty-handed."

She sighed and went on:

"They would have had nobody to turn to except the Elders who never had any money or at any rate far less than we had."

The Duke was touched by the way she had cared and Giovanna continued:

"They told me which Bank I could get in touch with in London or Edinburgh, and Grandmama said that her Solicitors who were in Naples would see to everything for me."

"Which I presume they did."

"Unfortunately they thought it was their business to write to my Stepmother, and I think it must have been their fault too that the news of my inheritance appeared first in the Italian newspapers and, as I learned later, was copied by the English, and I suspect the Scottish ones."

The Duke was sure that was what had happened and why both the Dalbeths and the McCarons had got in touch with the Marquess of Lothian as Secretary of State for Scotland.

"While I was finishing my time at the Convent I did not think very much about it after that," Giovanna said, "until I received a letter from Colonel Macbeth telling me I must return to Scotland and at the same time I also had a letter from Stepmama."

"What did she say?"

"She said that if my grandmother could arrange for me to be escorted as far as Dover, she would meet me there."

"Were you upset at the thought of seeing her again?"

"It seemed to be something that could not be helped,"

Giovanna replied. "I was only afraid that now Papa was dead she would be my Guardian, and I would have to obey her. But I knew that having so much money I would be able to do what I wanted as regards helping people, and I thought in that at any rate, I would be supported by my relations."

"So you left for Scotland."

"Grandmama talked to the Mother Superior and she sent one of the Nuns with me, a sweet Sister who had travelled quite a lot on behalf of the Convent to conferences or special meetings in Rome and places like that."

"And when you reached Dover—what then?"

"Stepmama and her elderly maid Annie, a woman I remembered but had never liked, were waiting for me at the Lord Warden Hotel. I said goodbye to the Nun and set off with them for Scotland."

The Duke waited, knowing this was the moment in her story where Giovanna began to be afraid.

"At first," she said shyly, "my Stepmother merely talked about my money and asked me what arrangements had been made about it. I saw no reason not to tell the truth and showed her all the letters and documents which Grandmama's Solicitors had handed to me before I left Naples."

She gave a sigh before she added:

"It was only later that I realised how foolish I had been. She now knew the names of the Bank Managers to be contacted in London or Edinburgh, who had promised to do anything I wished, and transfer money to any Bank in Scotland which would be convenient."

"And when did your Stepmother ask you to do that?"

"We stayed the night in London, where a Representative for the Bank came to the Hotel and I signed a lot of documents which Stepmother read very carefully before I did so."

As if the Duke was accusing her of being stupid, Giovanna said:

"She had been quite pleasant to me on the journey from Dover and I thought now I was older and Papa was dead, she did not seem to hate me as much as she had three years earlier. In fact, I believed she wanted to be friendly."

"I am sure she acted her part very well!" the Duke said sarcastically.

He did not however want to prevent Giovanna from telling him every detail and she continued:

"It was not until we had reached Inverness that my Stepmother came into the carriage where I had slept quite peacefully and said:

" 'We will have rather a rough drive before we reach home, and as the roads have been badly damaged by the winter rains I have brought you something to soothe your stomach. Personally I find the roughness of the roads worse than the waves of the sea!'

" 'You make it sound terrible!' I laughed trying to remember what the roads had been like when I had left home.

" 'We have had two very bad winters,' my Stepmother said, 'and one is thrown about the carriage from side to side until one feels quite sick and dizzy!'

" 'I shall be all right,' I laughed.

" 'Well, drink this anyway,' my Stepmother said, offering me a small glass filled with a white liquid.

" 'I would rather not,' I answered, 'I am sure it tastes nasty!'

" 'It merely tastes of peppermint,' she replied. 'I have made it up specially for you. I have just had some myself and given the same amount to Annie.' "

Giovanna moved a little closer to the Duke.

"I . . I know it was . . foolish of me, but she was so insistent and I did not . . want to upset her . . I . . I never thought she would do the same sort of thing to me that she had done to . . Papa.''

"What happened?"

"I . . I drank what she had given me . . and a few minutes later I must have . . fallen back unconscious for I can . . remember nothing of what happened after that.''

"You were drugged!" the Duke exclaimed.

"I must have been,'' Giovanna agreed, ''and it lasted all the way back. The next thing I knew . . I was lying on a bed . . in a room that when I lived at home had . . never been used.''

"You were alone?''

"I . . I was alone when I . . came back to consciousness and I felt . . desperately . . terribly ill. I managed to get off the bed . . and I found a tap and only as I attempted to fill a glass with some water did I . . realise where . . I was.''

"Where were you?''

"In a room that had been specially built onto the house by my grandfather for his mother.''

The Duke waited and Giovanna explained:

"She was very old and apparently had a horror of noise . . in fact even the slightest sound could keep her awake at night . . and so my grandfather built a special room on one of the top floors which was isolated from the rest of the house.''

She made a little gesture with her hand as she explained:

"In order to reach it one had to walk along two empty corridors. It fortunately had a bathroom attached and there was running water . . only cold of course . . but which I know now saved my life.''

"You mean because you could drink even if they did not feed you?''

Giovanna nodded.

"If I had been . . thirsty as well as hungry . . I am sure

129

I should have died quite quickly . . and being starved would have been . . more agonising even than . . it was.''

"When did you know what was happening to you?" the Duke asked.

"Stepmother came and told me. Then I knew how much she had always hated me when I was at home and that not only had her hatred grown stronger, but she loathed and detested me because I was rich.

'' 'If you think you can control your money,' she said, 'you are very much mistaken, and if you think you are going to marry a Duke as they have planned for you to do, you are also in for a surprise!'

'' 'What are you talking about?' I asked. 'This is the first I have heard that I am to be married.'

'' 'Apparently those old fools the Macbeths and the McCarons have decided you shall marry the Duke of Invercaron,' she said, 'and reign like a Queen in Scotland with all your money to spend! But I am going to stop it, and you are going to reign nowhere as far as I am concerned, except in Hell!'

'' 'I do not know . . what you are . . talking about,' I cried.

'' 'Then listen to me,' my Stepmother replied. 'What is going to happen to you is that you are going to die!'

'' 'I think you must be mad!' I said. 'Do you not suppose there will be questions asked as to where I am and what has happened to me? And as Chieftain my Clan will want to see me.' ''

Giovanna shuddered as she added:

"Then . . she smiled, and for the first time I was . . really frightened.

'' 'Your Clansmen will see you,' she said in a mocking voice. 'They will see their pretty Chieftain and they will applaud as she marries the Duke of Invercaron and throws her money about like confetti, but it will not be you—not poor mad Giovanna whom I brought to live here out of sheer kindness because she had nowhere else to go. No, Giovanna, you are going to die! A girl who is mad—deranged—suffering from fits of screaming and frenzy, which is dangerous! No one will mourn her when she is dead. She will just be pushed into the ground . . and . . forgotten!' "

As Giovanna finished speaking the tears choked her voice and she turned her face against the Duke's shoulder and he held her closer against him.

"I can understand, my precious darling, how terrifying it must have been," he said gently.

"I thought I must be imagining it, but it was . . true. She had it all planned and the only person who . . came near me was that horrible old Annie who had . . always hated me. She used to say through the door:

" 'I've brought ye a delicious dinner an' t'Cook's taken ever so much trouble o'er it. There's salmon fresh frae t'river, and venison so tender as it'll melt in ye're mouth, but it's mad ye are, ye puir wee thing, that ye jus' send it awa' untouched!' "

Giovanna gave a little gulp remembering what a nightmare it had been before she said:

"I . . I could . . hear Annie waiting . . until the food was cold . . before she carried the tray away again . . saying I was . . too mad and too . . ill to eat."

"I can hardly believe it!" the Duke exclaimed. "It seems incredible that such people really exist."

"It was . . terrifying!" Giovanna agreed. "And Stepmother used to come every other day to see how weak I was getting and to . . taunt me with what a . . success her daughter would be as the new Countess."

"Her daughter?" the Duke asked sharply. "Was it really her daughter?"

"I knew from what Papa said that she had been married before and she had one child . . but I never knew whether it was a boy or a girl . . until she said her daughter had taken my . . place and that nobody suspected for a . . moment that she was not . . me!''

Now the tears were running down Giovanna's face and the Duke kissed them away before he kissed her lips.

Then as he kissed her and went on kissing her he knew that only by the mercy of God had she survived the cruel fate that a demon in the shape of a woman had devised for her.

Chapter Seven

THE DUKE opened the door and Giovanna, who was sitting beside her grandmother and holding her hand, jumped to her feet.

There was an expression in her eyes which the Duke answered by crossing the room and putting his arms round her before he said quietly:

"Everything is arranged, but I do not want you to be frightened."

She moved a little nearer to him and he knew all she wanted was to hold onto him and feel that he was close to her.

He turned to Lady Sinclair saying:

"I have no wish for you to be upset, but I know you will understand that, while we are coping once and for all with these terrible people, one of the special police will have to sit here in the room with you."

Lady Sinclair did not answer and the Duke added:

"He is a very charming young man who speaks English, and I do not think he will embarrass you."

"You are not to worry about me," Lady Sinclair answered in a soft voice. "Just look after my grand-daughter."

"That is what I have sworn to do," the Duke replied.

Lady Sinclair put out her hand, and when he bent to kiss it in the foreign fashion Giovanna knew how much her grandmother liked him and how delighted she was that they were to be married.

Then the Duke drew Giovanna from the room and as he did so held the door open for the handsome young Italian Policeman who was to take their place.

Outside he took her into the largest Reception-Room in the Villa which to her surprise was empty.

"Now listen, my darling," the Duke said. "I am going to ask a great deal of you, but I want you to know that you are completely safe and protected and no-one can hurt you."

Giovanna looked at him in perplexity as he drew her to a sofa where they sat down together.

Outside the Mediterranean was dazzlingly blue, the garden was a riot of bougainvillaea, and the sky was cloudless.

It seemed incredible that they were menaced by such evil as might well have made everything dark around it.

When the Duke had approached the white Villa a few minutes before and thought how beautiful it was, he had known that both Giovanna's life and perhaps his, hung by a thread.

He looked at her now and said in a quiet voice which he hoped would reassure her:

"I am going to ask you, my precious darling, to be very brave."

"W . what do you . . want me to . . do?"

"As you know, I have been in consultation with the Chief of Police," the Duke said, "and he tells me that he knows all about Kane Horn, who is in fact, a criminal accountable for a number of murders. They have been trying to capture him for a long time. Not long ago they thought they had him trapped, but he slipped away at the last moment, and that is when he must have gone to Scotland."

"And . . my Stepmother . . . ?" Giovanna questioned.

"She is almost as bad as he is," the Duke replied. "But to convict them the Police must have incontrovertible proof of their wickedness and that is where you have to help."

Giovanna drew in her breath and after a moment said in a little voice that trembled:

"What are you . . asking me to . . do?"

"They have arrived in Naples and are on their way here at this moment," the Duke said calmly. "When they get here I want you to meet them."

Giovanna looked at him wide-eyed.

"A . . alone?"

"You will only appear to be alone," the Duke explained. "You will in fact, be protected not only by me but also by a number of the most highly-trained Police Officers in the whole of Italy."

He felt her fingers tighten on his and he said quickly:

"Kane Horn will not see them, and he will not know they are there until they have heard him threaten you. Then they will take over."

"But . . suppose he . . k . kills me?"

"Before he can pull the trigger he will die!" the Duke answered firmly.

He saw the fear in Giovanna's eyes and added:

"I know it is a lot to ask of you, my darling, but you you have been so brave, so courageous up to now, and I know you will understand that there is no other way in which these people can be disposed of for ever and punished for the crimes they have already committed."

"I . . I understand."

The Duke held her closer still and kissed her. Then he raised his head to say:

"I knew you would not fail me, and remember however frightened you may be, together we will be victorious!"

He did not wait for her reply but drew her to her feet saying:

"I think I hear the sound of wheels and I am therefore going to leave you. But I promise I am very near, my sweet, and I swear before God that no-one shall harm a hair of your lovely head!"

He kissed her again and as there was the sound of voices outside the front door he moved swiftly behind a screen which was across one corner of the room.

Giovanna appeared to be alone, but there were in fact, armed policemen concealed behind the curtains and other pieces of furniture in the room.

One of the Chief's men had left the house five minutes before, dressed in the Duke's clothes and top-hat, and driving in an open carriage which belonged to Lady Sinclair.

The Duke knew he would pass Kane Horn and his assassins on the coast road leading back into Naples and it was most unlikely they would suspect that the man who appeared to be the Duke could be anybody else.

Everything had been planned down to the very last detail, but it was impossible for the Duke hiding behind a very ornate Chinese screen not to be afraid for Giovanna.

At the same time he felt great admiration for the way in which she had accepted what he had asked of her without argumemt and without complaint.

He knew it was her Scottish blood which made her stand waiting with her chin up, her eyes on the door which led into the marble hall.

There was the sound of footsteps, then the door opened and Kane Horn stood there.

There was an expression of satisfaction on his face

when he saw Giovanna apparently alone and waiting for him. Arrogantly he walked into the room followed by two men who, she thought, were those who had been with him at the Castle.

Then to her surprise she saw there was yet another man much older with a grey beard and wearing a cassock.

Kane Horn walked slowly towards Giovanna and only when he was a few feet away from her did he speak and say:

"I imagine, as the Duke has left you here alone, you were not expecting to see me so soon. It was clever of you to get away, but you cannot escape again. As you see, I am here!"

"What do you want?" Giovanna asked.

Although her voice was low there was not a tremor in it.

"That is something I am going to explain to you," Kane Horn replied.

At that moment there was the sound from the hall of a woman's voice loud and shrill.

There was no mistaking the surprise on Horn's face as a second later the door was flung open and the Dowager Countess burst into the room.

She was as over-dressed as usual, in a frilled and flowered gown and a Sable stole round her shoulders.

With an air both of fury and of defiance she swept across the room to face Kane Horn.

"What are you doing here?" he asked angrily. "I told you to wait for me at the Hotel!"

"I know you did," the Dowager Countess retorted, "but I wanted to be 'in at the kill', and why shouldn't I be?"

"Because you should have obeyed my orders!" he answered. "There will, in fact, be no kill!"

The Dowager Countess looked at him in astonishment.

"What do you mean?" she enquired. "You told me

you were going to kill the girl, and you know as well as I do that she has to die!''

Kane Horn did not reply and she went on, her voice rising.

''After all we have been through, why are you taking so long about it? Only when she is dead can we be certain there will be no more trouble, and her fortune will be in our hands!''

She spoke so menacingly that, hidden behind the screen, the Duke was afraid that Giovanna might lose her nerve and run away.

Instead she stood looking steadily at the woman who had married her father and who hated her with a hatred that was not only murderous but fanatical.

''If you had done what I told you to do,'' Kane Horn retorted, ''you would have learnt later without this quite unnecessary scene that I have changed my mind.''

''Changed your mind?'' the Dowager Countess screamed. ''What do you mean—changed your mind? You came here to kill her, and here she is alone except for the old woman. I passed the Duke on the road, as I suspect you did too. Kill her, and let us get away before anyone finds the body!''

The Dowager Countess's voice was vehement and rang out with a passion which told the Duke as he listened that she had lost all self-control and was on the verge of madness.

As if Kane Horn thought the same thing, he said furiously:

''Will you be quiet! What I've decided, and I'm not having you or anybody else interfering in my plans, is that I'll not kill this girl whom you were unable to destroy with your much-vaunted poison. Instead I intend to marry her!''

For a moment the Dowager Countess was so startled that her mouth fell open in astonishment, and she stared

138

at Kane Horn as if she could not have heard him aright.

As she was unable to speak he went on:

"I shall marry her, and I've brought a Priest here with me in order to perform the ceremony. After that there will be no need to dispose of a body. Her fortune'll be in my hands for all time!"

For the first time there was a warm note in his voice as if the idea gave him a great deal of satisfaction, but the Dowager Countess gave a shriek that seemed to echo round the room.

"You double-crossing rat!" she screamed. "You promised to marry me! Do you think after all you have said that I would let you marry anyone else?"

As she spoke, with a swiftness which could only have come from long practice, she drew a revolver from the satin handbag which she carried over one arm and shot Kane Horn through the heart.

The explosion was deafening, and almost simultaneously one of the men standing behind Horn fired a gun directly at her, and the bullet entered her neck just below her chin.

The same moment, almost before either she or Kane Horn could fall to the ground, the Duke had lifted Giovanna up in his arms and carried her from the room.

He had a glimpse as he went of the Police swarming from their various hiding-places, and he knew that it was all over.

It seemed very unlikely that either the Dowager Countess or Kane Horn would live even for a few minutes.

He carried Giovanna out through an open window onto the verandah.

There was a seat looking over the garden filled with flowers and cypress trees, and he put her down on the cushions, still holding her very tightly against him.

She hid her face but he realised she was not crying,

only shocked to the point where it was difficult to feel anything.

He kissed her forehead and smoothed the softness of her hair with his hand as he said:

"It is all over, my precious, you are free and all we have to decide now is how quickly you will marry me."

She did not reply, but only moved a little closer to him as if she wanted to be sure he was there and knew it was the only way she could be safe.

"You were very brave and very, very wonderful," he went on, "and I am extremely proud of you!"

She lifted her face to his and for a long moment he looked down at her, knowing they had fought a desperate battle against the evil that encroached on them both and had won.

Then slowly, as if now there was no hurry and they had all their lives in front of them, he bent his head and his lips found hers.

Only when he had kissed her with a long, gentle, possessive kiss did Giovanna say in a strange, incoherent little voice:

"Is . . is it . . really over . . and can I really . . be your w . wife?"

"As quickly as it is possible!" the Duke replied. "After that, my darling, you will be mine and nothing like this shall ever happen to you again."

Then as if he was frightened that he might have lost her he was kissing her demandingly, passionately, fiercely, as if only love could sweep away the terror she had been through.

*   *   *

Quite a long time later, when they were sure the Police would have left the Villa with the dead bodies, they went to find Lady Sinclair.

"You are . . all right, Grandmama?" Giovanna asked as they entered her room to find her sitting serenely in the same chair in which they had left her.

"Perfectly all right, my dearest," Lady Sinclair smiled, "and the Chief of Police has told me how splendid you were, and how grateful he is to you. He actually said that Naples will now be a happier and cleaner place without those fiends!"

Giovanna did not answer, she only looked at the Duke and he put his arm around her as he said:

"Now I have another problem for you, Lady Sinclair, which is how quickly we can be married. You will understand that Giovanna does not wish to be alone either by day or night, nor do I wish that either."

"Of course," Lady Sinclair agreed, "and because the British Consul is a very old friend of mine, I know he will make the way easy for you. And I have a suggestion regarding your honeymoon."

"Our . . honeymoon!" Giovanna murmured almost beneath her breath.

"What is it?" the Duke asked.

"I have a great friend, the Count Roberto Caruso, who has a Villa about half-a-mile from here. It is very beautiful with a most exquisite garden. He is away at the moment, but he asked me to look after the Villa in his absence, and I know nothing would give him greater pleasure than that you should stay there for your honeymoon. If there is anything else you want, you have only to ask me."

"It sounds too . . too . . wonderful!" Giovanna cried.

Then as if this combined with her relief after all she had been through had finally proved too much for her, the tears ran down her face as the Duke took her into his arms.

*   *   *

Giovanna awoke and realised that someone, and she knew who it was, had pulled back the curtains from the huge window which covered one wall of their bedroom.

Then as she saw the sun rising like a disc of gold, she felt her husband's arms go round her as he drew her close against him.

"This is the dawn of a new life, my precious little wife," he said. "I thought we should watch it together and know that from this moment everything has changed for us both."

"I am so . . happy!" Giovanna whispered. "I think perhaps I am . . dreaming."

"We are going to dream together," he said quietly, "not in the darkness any more, but in the sunshine!"

She knew exactly what he was saying to her and she turned so that she could be a little nearer to him and lifted her lips to his.

The British Consul who was very sympathetic had arranged for them to be married with almost unlawful speed, and they had driven from the British Church attached to the Consulate back to the Count's Villa where the servants had decorated all the rooms with white flowers.

The Duke had been half-afraid that after the long journey and everything she had been through Giovanna might collapse.

Instead she seemed to radiate with a new vitality, and he was aware that it was because she loved him so much that nothing else was of any importance.

He did not speak of it, but he half-believed that she had already forgotten the horror of seeing Kane Horn and her Stepmother die in front of her eyes.

He had known that it was a perfect solution to their problems for now there need be no trial, which would have involved unpleasant publicity and when they returned to Scotland the Dowager Countess's daughter

142

would presumably disappear and her attempt to pose as Giovanna would soon be forgotten.

The Duke had already written to Sir Iain McCaron explaining briefly what had occurred and asking him to inform the Dalbeth relations and to try to keep what had happened as secret as possible, and especially out of the newspapers.

Fortunately, as his own Castle and Dalbeth House were both so far away in the North it was unlikely the story would percolate to the South.

He could only pray that from now on they could live a quiet, normal life without any more dramatics.

Later in the evening she had asked him:

"Are you going to go on calling me Giovanna?"

Because he could read her thoughts, the Duke knew she would always connect 'Jane' with the girl who had impersonated her.

"To me," he replied, "Giovanna is the loveliest name in the world and I shall never change it."

She gave a deep sigh and murmured:

"That is what I wanted you to say."

Last night after their wedding when he had been able to tell Giovanna of his love, the ecstasy and rapture he had evoked in her made the Duke feel he had reached a special Heaven he had never known existed.

He had been very gentle and very controlled in making love to Giovanna, because he had known that she still had a long way to go before she was really well again, and also he was afraid of shocking her.

As he suspected she was very innocent, but because she loved him, the ecstasy they had known when he first kissed her was multiplied and intensified until the Duke thought they both reached the glory of the Divine.

It was different from anything he had ever known in his whole life, while to Giovanna it was a revelation.

"I love you . . I love you!" she whispered. "Why did

nobody . . tell me that . . love was as wonderful as . . this?''

"I have made you happy, my darling?"

"I am so happy that I think I must have . . died! No one could be alive and . . feel as I do!"

The Duke laughed and it was a very tender sound.

"You are alive, my adorable one, I am holding you close against me, and you are my wife."

"It is . . true . . it is . . really true," she whispered as if she must convince herself.

"It may take years to convince you," the Duke replied, "but every day I shall love you more and kiss more of your soft beautiful body."

He knew she blushed as she said:

"I am . . ugly because I am so . . thin."

"You are beautiful," the Duke said positively, "and I am looking at you not only with my eyes but with my spirit and my soul."

He laughed softly.

"You know exactly what I am trying to say because we are both Scots and both 'fey'. It is what we feel that matters, and what I feel about you can only be written by the light of the stars and the burning rays of the sun."

"How can you say such . . wonderful things to me?" Giovanna cried in a broken little voice.

There were really no words to do justice to his feelings, so the Duke only kissed her until the flames of love burnt like the sun through them both.

When Giovanna had fallen asleep he had lain awake for a long time thanking God that he had found anything so perfect, and dedicating himself now and for all time to making her happy.

He had known it was absolutely true that if she had not had a penny to her name he would have married her because they belonged to each other not only physically but spiritually and mentally.

But to know he was, as he thought, the happiest man in the world, and also able now to do so much for the Clansmen who looked up to them both for protection and guidance was a joy which made him sure that their future together was going to be very wonderful.

Now, looking at Giovanna's eyes as she stared at the sunrise, he knew she was not only the most exciting woman he had ever known in his life, but also the most beautiful.

It was not only her features or even the loveliness of her eyes, it was her sensitivity, her compassion and above all her courage which made her different from anybody else he had ever known.

He knew too that since, as he had said last night, they were both 'fey' with an instinct for what was right and wrong, combined with his powers of prescience which had not only saved him in the past but would enrich his life and Giovanna's in the future, they were unique.

"We have so much," he told himself.

As if she knew what he was thinking, Giovanna turned towards him with a little smile and asked:

"Are you feeling grateful that we are here . . together and that you saved me from dying at the cascade?"

"You are not to speak of it again!" the Duke answered. "That is all in the past, and I was thinking of the future and how much we will do for those who trust us."

"I have been thinking of that too," she said, "and I know that you will not only help our people at home, but also the whole of Scotland. Mama often said that what the Scots needed was a leader to speak for us not only in England but in Europe."

The Duke smiled as he asked her:

"Is that what you want me to do?" the Duke asked.

"I believe it is what you will do," Giovanna said softly.

He kissed her then because it was what he wanted to hear.

It was a gentle kiss of love, but the softness of her lips, the nearness of her body against his, and the vibrations which united them once again made him feel the fires of the sun burning within him.

Then he knew as Giovanna quivered against him that she was feeling the same.

"I love you!" the Duke said. "My darling, my precious, perfect, wonderful little wife, I love you so desperately that I can never be grateful enough for having found you."

"I love you . . until you . . fill the whole world," Giovanna said, "and there is nothing else in life . . but you!"

The way she spoke was very moving.

As the Duke was kissing her passionately, demandingly, her heart beating beneath his, the rising sun shone through the windows enveloping them with a dazzling light.

It was an emblem of their love and also of the power which would always ensure that eventually good could overcome evil.

"I love you!" the Duke said again.

"Love me! Oh, darling, wonderful Talbot . . love me," Giovanna whispered.

Then there was only the gold of the sun and love which is life itself in all its glory.